William Gerard

Byron Re-Studied in his Dramas

being a contribution towards a definitive estimate of his genius - an essay

William Gerard

Byron Re-Studied in his Dramas
being a contribution towards a definitive estimate of his genius - an essay

ISBN/EAN: 9783337303280

Printed in Europe, USA, Canada, Australia, Japan

Cover: Foto ©Andreas Hilbeck / pixelio.de

More available books at **www.hansebooks.com**

BYRON

RE-STUDIED IN HIS DRAMAS;

BEING A CONTRIBUTION TOWARDS A DEFINITIVE
ESTIMATE OF HIS GENIUS.

AN ESSAY

BY

WILLIAM GERARD.

LONDON:

F. V. WHITE & CO.,
31, SOUTHAMPTON STREET, STRAND, W.C.

1886.

" Our Byron was in his youth but what Schiller and Goethe had been in theirs. . . . With longer life, all things were to have been hoped for from Byron ; for he loved truth in his inmost heart, and would have discovered at last that his Corsairs and Harolds were not true. It was otherwise appointed. But with one man all hope does not die. If this way is the right one, we too shall find it."

Carlyle (in 1827).

" Charm is the glory which makes
Song of the poet divine,
Love is the fountain of charm.
How without charm wilt thou draw,
Poet ! the world to thy way ?

Charm is the poet's alone."

M. Arnold.

" Δεῖ με νῦν καθεύδειν."

Byron's last words.

SUMMARY.

———◆———

I

II.

III.

IV.

V.

Presence in the Dramas of an elemental power—What this implies—Universality defined—Its possession not incompatible with a marked individuality—Its operation to be continuously traced in Byron's work—The genius of Byron one in kind with that of Shakespeare—Relative force of the personal element in Byron, in Shakespeare, and in Goethe—Universality in its creative aspect—The Dramas of Byron, like those of Shakespeare, are a vast potentiality—Their natural evolution—Their homogeneity—Dramatic morality—How far this is conditioned in Byron by his special method—Byron's dramatization compared with that of Shakespeare—His characters—The Protagonist—The Woman—The minor characters—Byron's imagination—The nature of its limitations—Byron's imagination implies a basis of thought—Charm as the ideal effect of imagination 141—196

VI.

The Dramas reveal the highest tendency of Byron's genius—Approach to a final definition—This tested by a comparison of Byron with some poets of all time; with his English cotemporaries; with Shelley, Coleridge, Keats; with foreign

BYRON RE-STUDIED IN HIS DRAMAS.

I.

THE work of every great poet may be said to undergo certain inevitable transformations before assuming its final form. There is first that earliest stage of change and growth, during which it suffers the untempered criticism of cotemporary praise or blame; a second, when, chrysalis-like, it seems partially obscured and withdrawn from sight, as a colder reflection brings its estimate to bear and the forces of reaction and oblivion begin to work; and a third and final one, when, born anew as it were under the calm judgment of posterity, it issues perfect to the light and is seen in definite relation to its time and to literature in general.

That for Byron this final consummation should have seemed to come but late is no more than was naturally to be expected in the case of a writer so extraordinary and a work so exaggerated both in excellence and defect. About qualities such as these the world was quickly agreed; yet there remained always the more danger that it was resting content with a half-truth after all, and thinking that it knew Byron when in reality it did not know him. From the first his faults were apotheosized in the works of his imitators and the crude appreciation of the general public, while his better part slept with him, untouched by the Ithuriel's spear of criticism. Byronism, in fact, became confused for posterity with Byron, an error as uncritical in kind as would be the identification of Werther with Goethe. Nor can we even yet claim to be free from the consequences of this error. Not only has the superficial Byron posed before the world so long, but he has touched so many responsive chords in the hearts of other than his own countrymen, has centred in himself an interest so varied and intense, that criticism too has felt its glance dazzled and has hesitated to pronounce its final verdict. To the perplexity attending the man and his work is now added the complication wrought by time; for the full recognition of his genius has been delayed until an atmosphere of thought quite other than that in which he wrote has supervened, and a cycle of poets, whose work is in sharpest contrast with his own, has almost run its course. From this confused mist of lights and shadows the form of the true Byron begins slowly to emerge. That earliest grotesque phantom of it is laid for ever. Those mysterious effigies of Lara or of Harold, splendid alike in sin and sorrow, loom faded in the world of thought like the figures of some ancient wall-painting. Or, to change the point of view, the vulgar mystery of *Manfred*, the supposed irreligiousness of *Cain*, touch no fibre in this scientific but nowise unpoetic or irreligious age. As the earlier glow fades we become conscious, nearer to our own day, of inevitable detracting voices, unmeasured, anything but criti-

cal, which speak of a Byron strangely attenuated
and changed indeed—an unlovely Byron, who
was no less weak as a poet than he was bad as
a man—a rhetorician with some rude force but
no real genius, theatrical, insincere—a barbarian,
in short, devoid of taste, devoid of art, devoid of
imagination. Uncritical as were these attacks,
they were at least useful in stripping the tinsel
from what was a lay-figure, and so demonstrating
its unreality. Only quite lately have critics, both
native and foreign, of wider range and insight,
sympathetic but discriminating, not led into extremes, "without illusion," come forth to show
us the reality—a man Byron, deeply erring but
human and noble; a poet Byron, with terrible
faults but of great if dubitable genius (i.). These
judgments, by re-sifting and accentuating the
actual details, and by concentrating the issues

(i.) It is necessary, in order to avoid misconception, to state that
these words were written before the appearance of Mr. Swinburne's
essay on Wordsworth and Byron, in which apparently he reverses
the verdict of an earlier essay on Byron. His later essay, however,
as being essentially a polemic, hardly falls within range of the
criticism contemplated in this study.

involved, have minimized the force of any misconceptions tending to blur the true features of Byron. Substantially, and as regards the elemental facts, they render that impression of him which posterity will probably be content to adopt —an impression which no fresh details of his life and character can now materially affect. After a long and dubious trial, in which all his former pretensions have been challenged, he has been allowed to put on his singing robes and to take his place among the immortal poets, his peers. But only as it were on sufferance. His fame does not rest assured on both a critical and popular basis as the fame of Shakespeare or of Milton rests assured.

As one reads and re-reads the judgment of Byron's latest and wisest critics it seems to give forth an uncertain sound. For previous misconceptions it substitutes a misconception greater still. It speaks of particular faults and particular merits, but does not harmonize these discrepancies under a wider conception or clearly trace their relation to the genius underlying them; while it leaves the nature of that genius too much a matter of inference, and, as a consequence, bases the fame of the poet on a foundation that appears still shifting, still unstable. Is it necessary to rest in this uncertainty? If, indeed, Byron had written only poetry, the answer might be given in the affirmative; though even so there would still be need for a warning word. If the defence of Byron's mere style cannot be based on some general principle, his fame remains vitiated at its source. Of this, however, there will be occasion to speak more fully presently. But Byron wrote not poetry only, but drama, and it is here that even his best critics would seem to lie open to the charge, not of total want of insight, but of negligence—as of generals who, in setting out their critical array, leave unoccupied a coign of vantage that would enable them at least to press their investigation from a more commanding eminence and to a more satisfactory issue.

Assuredly the present writer is under no spell

of Byronism. Rather he had, at starting, to strive against haunting adverse prepossessions: still it has seemed to him that for yet another attempt, and from the vantage-ground here indicated, there is even now room. Criticism, growing graver with the times, must deign more and more to become the study of relations, and renouncing her crisp and sparkling judgments, adjust her glances to wider horizons. A distinguished writer (ii.) has lately shown with fruitful effect how the most prominent facts of history may be misread, and how necessary it may be, in the light of later knowledge and with a view to future action, to subject them afresh to consideration. Or if illustrations be sought in a sphere more cognate to our subject, they may be found in the second part of *Faust*, the living existence of which is but now dawning on the slowly-wakened perception of the world; or in Shake-speare himself and his dramatic peers, whose works required fully all these centuries and a

(ii.) Professor Seeley: " Expansion of England."

favourable epoch for their giant proportions to be seen in true perspective.

Is it too late, at a moment when his greatness still hangs in question, to apply this method to Byron, in whom what is superficial so dazzles and misleads? I have said that as to the main facts about him the world is agreed; but the meaning, the significance of those facts, the law that embraces them and in which they cohere is still veiled in the mists of controversy. Any investigation, therefore, must proceed, not on the lines of attempting to discover something new and startling, but of so emphasizing some known results too lightly touched upon, and bringing out others, perhaps not yet touched upon at all, as to give unity to a picture of the poet's mind in which the critical and popular appreciation may rest. And here we receive some unexpected help and the promise of a guiding hand hitherto not sufficiently regarded. For it seems very probable that a right understanding of Goethe's famous judgment, accepted in its full and natural sense, may lead us precisely to the definition of which we are in quest; and if we can further demonstrate the affinities by virtue of which Byron reaches forward to Goethe himself and the modern era, backwards to Shakespeare and the Greeks, we shall have succeeded in vindicating his title to a fame based not on the sands of emotional judgment but the rock of firmly-ordered evidence (iii.). Let us at least make the endeavour, and allowing the critical imagination to range freely as it lists, without prejudice, seek to penetrate through Byronism to the central genius that was Byron ; choosing, indeed, the dramas as his richest seed-plot, but advancing through and from them to a principle that shall be found to underlie his work as a whole. Perhaps a criticism that is content to listen may discern under the more glaring discords the finer music

---

(iii.) I would here record a special obligation to Mr. M. Arnold, who has re-discussed the significance of Goethe's criticism on Byron ; and to M. Taine, who has considered the relation of Byron to Goethe in a comparison of *Manfred* with *Faust*. The present essay, however, besides being worked out on independent lines, reaches also a conclusion differing from theirs.

that endures. It is true that the chief characteristics of Byron's poetry re-appear in the dramas,
but they re-appear with a difference. Herein
lies the possibility of new discoveries. Beginning
with truisms, we may find them enlarging into
new truths; committing ourselves to the well-
beaten tracks, we may find them gradually di-
verging and leading us to fresh vistas. The
dramas have long been studied merely in the
light of the poetry; it may be well worth while,
after comparing the points which both share in
common, to consider whether some elements do
not remain in the dramatic which are wanting to
the poetical work. In those elements may be
found the harmonizing conception of which we
are in search ; and this again may reflect fresh
light on the poet's work as a whole.

What then, to begin with, were those master-
strands in the poetry of Byron which we are to
expect, yet changed, yet with a difference, in his
dramas? Barely enumerated they are: the note
of Humanity, the note of Revolt, the note of

Nature.   Elaborated, they form the complete gamut of his lyre, the musical expression of those ideas which in their combination and interaction constitute his very genius.   The humanity of Byron is world-embracing.   The earth is the smallest stage he deigns to regard, mankind the only nation.   Of times, of periods he recks not; all history must unfold her page before him that he may select where he will her manifestations of the human spirit.   And this he does not meditatively nor subtly (for he was not " Goethe nor another "), but with a forceful impatience that seizes upon the broad features and disdains all minor gradations.   Yet his treatment is always great, and the sympathetic grasp of his genius so commanding that this " barbarian " has flashed before us gleams of the " glory that was Athens and the grandeur that was Rome," such as are reflected in the verse of no other poet.   And his sympathy has nothing in it narrow or partial, but is universal, pulsing as strongly for the poorest as the noblest, for man as oppressed by his fellow-man or by inevitable fate or harsher circumstance. Only in one aspect is human nature abhorrent to him—as it is untrue to itself and so inhuman. The spectacle of man's cruelty, falseness, insincerity, conventionality, turns his sympathy to its natural obverse of hatred, and stings all his nature to revolt. When humanity has put on this inhumanity, when what might be so noble appears so base, what is left but to hurl down this idol of clay that aped godhead? So is born Byron's terrible satire. Strong in the immutable strength of its truth, and wrought by the bitterness of its righteous indignation to a more than human precision of severity, an artistic symmetry of sarcasm, his satire at its highest becomes a divine winged lightning, scathing and annihilating its object. But when emotion has subsided, how shall Byron arraign his fellow-man? For is there not in himself too, marred as he is by cruel circumstance and impotency of will, a consciousness of inherent weakness which paralyzes his tongue? Let man and his vileness go by, and a new world

open in woman, with her boundless capacities of
sympathy and love.   So Byron resigns himself
naïvely to this lovely phantom, and as he ex-
perienced, so he delineates with pulsing energy
every phase of passion as it floods and ebbs.   And
even as passion palls, lo! a still fresh pursuit.
Though man delight him not, nor woman neither,
there unrolls itself before him the whole pageant
of this petty life—a sight for infinite jest, a
laughable, amusing puppet-show—wherein with
inconceivable contortions, as the whim of their
vain folly or ambition prompts them, the human
mannikins play their fantastic parts.   Here at
last no illusion is possible, and Byron, with
mocking lips and a strange light of irony in his
eyes, takes up the multitudinous, fascinating, endless tale, which fails only as he from time to
time looks away from it and lays down his jaded
pen, and which, alternated only by passing outbursts of scorn and haunted by a recurring
ground-note of elegiac sorrow, closes only with
his life.   But in the pauses trouble and anguish

still lay hold upon his soul. This medley of all he has seen and suffered so appals him that he is fain to turn from earth to heaven, if haply he may find there some certain solution of the monstrous riddle of the universe. Only when heaven itself remains silent does the poet of humanity abate hope. Then mankind, the world, life itself, fade to pure negation, and there is nothing left remarkable beneath the moon. Henceforth, till death end all, he will fall back upon *himself*, and because the yearnings of his gigantic sympathy still remain unappeased, throw himself on the breast of Nature, contemplate her every aspect, meditate her every mystery, commune with her heart to heart, nay more, rise to identification with her, until his spirit, disembodied of the burden of the flesh, be one with hers (iv.).

These are the more striking antitheses which on a casual perusal of his poetry disclose themselves, not without an effect of bewildering confusion,

(iv.) Cf. *Childe Harold*, iii. 73—75.

to the ordinary reader of Byron, but the significant interdependence of which has not, perhaps, been fully understood. There is a stanza in *Childe Harold* which may help to make this clear. The poet is floating in his boat on the Lake of Geneva, and it is "the hush of night," when "all is concentered in a life intense." "Then," says Byron:

> " Then stirs the feeling infinite, so felt
>   In solitude, where we are *least* alone ;
>   A truth, which through our being then doth melt
>   And purifies from self : it is a tone,
>   The soul and source of music, which makes known
>   Eternal harmony, and sheds a charm,
>   Like to the fabled Cytherea's zone,
>   Binding all things with beauty ;—'twould disarm
> The spectre Death, had he substantial power to harm" (v.).

This remarkable passage, which resumes the essence of innumerable others expressive of the repose and refreshment that Nature yields, affords a microcosm, as it were, of the poet's soul, with all its jarring contradictions resolved into a higher

(v.) *Ibid.*, iii. 90.

unity. Antæus-like, he has thrown himself upon
the breast of the universal mother, and in that
abandonment found not only rest but restored
strength. Nature, sought only as the balm to
soothe the wounds inflicted by human strife, an
anodyne to assuage the pangs of a diseased self,
is found to be the oracle of the mystery of life.
Her touch, restorative upon his soul, purges also
his eyes, revealing to him an infinite Spirit, in
which his own moves and has its being as a
brother amongst brothers, an "eternal harmony,"
towards which the vain strivings of his rebellion
are but a confused aspiration. The persistency of
Byron's recoil from man to nature lays its stress
on the rebound of the antithesis. The harmony
he found in nature only Byron would gladly have
sought in the world; and although he knows that
the weakness which is his fate for ever forbids
the realization of his ideal, this remains with
him as the haunting dream of what might have
been. Nature receives him always as a poet
of revolt to restore him to us as the poet of

humanity (vi.). Humanity!—that is the potent word, the invisible bridge that leads us without sense of transition from the lyric Byron to Byron the dramatic poet, shaping passion into action.

(vi.) Cf. *Childe Harold*, iv. 178: "I love not man the less, but nature more," &c.

II.

THE passage still, however, remains to be made. Some effort is needed to disentangle the dramas from the poetry. Byron, we know, suffers from his affluence. His poetry, in its imposing mass and greater attractiveness, overpowers his dramatic efforts, and casts over them, for the reader already sated by superabundance, the prejudicial shadows of too probable defects little likely to be out-weighed by dubious excellences. Yet if Byron had never written a line of poetry, his dramas would be too important to be overlooked, and, though shorn of a commentary that powerfully illuminates them, would have shone with their own unborrowed light, a serener, milder galaxy. Still their true interest lies in being considered a part of Byron's whole work, and, judged thus, they would weigh not lightly in the scale, if only as the counterpart of the poetry. Comparatively dull,

heavy and tedious, they afford an outlet to that
sadder, more solemn and serious mood of Byron's
genius which does not elsewhere find identical
expression, but differs by a shade no less from the
sæva indignatio of his satire, the gloom of his
meditative poetry, and the passionate vivacity of
his narrative verse, than from the rippling grace
of his lighter and more mocking style. Allowing
for the moment that Cain and Manfred and Arnold
are but the pourtrayal in a different guise of the
personality that animates Harold or Conrad or
Juan, they at least accentuate the features of the
portrait, and add a completeness it would otherwise lack. But how little is this compared to
what we might naturally expect when a poet such
as Byron attempts the dramatic form! Dramatic
poetry, when not a mere fiasco, when possessed
of any consistency, however slight, compels the
writer to an intenser and more concentrated mode
of expression. If he display only himself he must
do so with an implied reference to dramatic laws
and within the limitations exacted by dramatic

form. And the greater the writer the more interesting this dramatic presentment of his being (vii.). Byron loved to compare himself to Napoleon; and there is more in the comparison than he himself was probably aware of. The impetuous rhetoric force, the lack of artistic restraint in the poet, are the analogue of the mechanical will, the vulgarity of the soldier. But Byron as poet resembles Napoleon at St. Helena, gloomily contemplating from afar the world he has lost, or living o'er again the struggle in the bare recital; while Byron as dramatist is Napoleon in the field, living a " being more intense " as a part of that which he creates, and revealed in action a moving, incarnate force. And even though the limbs of this would-be Achilles girding himself for sterner contests and on other plains than Troy should not be strong enough to bear dramatic armour, his efforts to assume it would be interesting. His contortions here would teach us the better to measure his prowess elsewhere. But still more

(vii.) See Note at end of this essay.

interesting, in the light of those general allusions and assertions and counter-assertions of friend and foe, do the dramas become when considered as a battlefield on which might finally be decided those crucial questions which critics still seem content to answer obscurely—leaving them as neither wholly denied nor resolutely confirmed, not altogether unsolved nor yet clearly solved—turning from them "with half-shut eyes as in a dream." How far is it true that Byron pourtrayed only himself? Had his genius, with all its admitted power and variety, any touch of that deeper quality which could be termed in any sense dramatic? Does this self-concentrated poet really come, whether in promise or actual performance, next to Shakespeare, the myriad-minded? Is there any groundwork of truth for those utterances of cotemporary criticism, at first sight so extravagant, which declared him in certain passages to have equalled or surpassed on their own ground such mighty and diverse masters as Æschylus, Milton, Goethe.

Meanwhile there are certain characteristics which, being common both to the poetical and the dramatic work, must be considered before the latter can be treated on its essential merits. To the fastidious and discriminating criticism of to-day the head and front of Byron's offending is his style (viii.). As so much hinges on the charge, and as even the warmest defenders of his poetry leave him in too equivocal a position with regard to it, some general discussion of this point may be permissible to the advocate of his dramatic power.

The style is the man, the unerring index of the genius; but it may be read improperly. Byron's style is his work as a whole, and has been misconceived as Byron himself has been misconceived. Nothing is to be said against the keen and penetrating acumen of our best modern criticism nor the refined, æsthetic poetry, without which for a theme it could not have gained such perfection as

(viii.) I refer of course to the general development of criticism in the hands of a few great and considerable writers, not ironically to our current journeyman criticism.

an instrument; but if there is no higher unity that
embraces the art of Tennyson and the energy
of Byron, criticism must retrace its steps to find
it. Of all magic that could be conferred by art
in its stricter sense, Byron's poetry is indeed
dark and void. His style knows nothing of such
added comeliness. It has no felicities of diction,
no Virgilian words weighted with remembered
beauty. And no severity of form compensates
for the lacking charm. Nothing but the un-
sleeping force seems to uphold the thought flung
out haughtily at random and the crude beauty
scattered broadcast. But be its defects what they
may, Byron's style can more than prove its right
of place; it is even beneficial as a protest against
what is weak, extravagant and affected in the
style opposed to it. Some such bold, untram-
melled voice is needed now and again to show
us that poetry is an inspiration as well as an
art—a bright, informing spirit working from
within, that tends to clothe itself in beautiful
forms, but that does not invariably so clothe

itself.   A perfect genius would find expression
in perfect verse; but where all fall short of the
ideal, defects are comparative ; and Byron's qualities
can bear the strain of his defects.   His un-
musicalness is no more and no less a fault than
is the ruggedness of Browning ; in both a defect,
a falling-short to be regretted, a sign of interior
weakness, it is yet in both upborne by their
genius, that beats against its limitations.   How
careless is that criticism of Byron that hastes
to reduce his poetry once and for all to rhetoric !
This is to confound the aberrations of a faculty
with the faculty itself.   It was in vain for Byron
to despise Art, and to drag her, naked and dis-
hevelled, with bruised and bleeding limbs, behind
his rushing chariot.   There were times when she
asserted her unconscious sway and took the reins
from his hands.   At such halcyon moments a
higher inspiration carries him as it were away
with it and sustains him at its own height.
Then the idea rising luminous and clear within
him impresses on the surging volume of his

utterance an answering comeliness of form. The words take some magic as they melt into lines; the lines harmonious flow into rhythms; the rhythms swell to cadences, and the lofty verse thus built up renders a creative effect breathing the piercing sincerity, the absolute simplicity of great poetry—resonant with no selfish agitation of the singer, but with the larger appropriate emotion that abides.

Such passages, in their entirety, are rare in Byron, though he often approaches them; but they mark the height he attained—a perfection towards which his whole style was a constant tendency. To those who will listen largely, Byron's rude, impetuous note is ever trembling on the verge of true music. His style, in short, is a great style maimed and marred, sometimes beyond recognition, like the man himself; but it never is—what some would make it—that very different thing, a false style, reflecting with hollow pompousness and mean magniloquence a mind unpoetic and insincere.

If we apply this distinction more particularly
to his dramatic style, his failure and his success
appear the greater as the drama is the higher
form of art. As his poetry lacks Virgilian sweet-
ness and modern subtlety, so his dramatic verse
is bare of Elizabethan largeness and splendour.
The maledictions which criticism has heaped upon
the Byronian tragic metre may be summed up
in a Virgilian line. At the first aspect we
salute it as akin to that

" Monstrum horrendum informe ingens cui *lumen* ademptum."

The *eye* of any style, nervously adapting itself
to express the fulness of the inward vision, is
indeed conspicuously absent, on a superficial
glance, from this shapeless structure of metre.
External evidences of its unlovely poverty are
at once afforded by the recurrent mannerisms
that deface every page—the despicable device
of aposiopesis, the abuse of italics, the distortion
and affectation of the phraseology; while deeper
indications of it appear in the doggerel colloca-

tions of words and sentences, in the structure-
less deformity of passages from which rhythm
and proportion are banished, and in the rhetorical
cast of the expression, which too often does duty
for naturalness of speech and the true accent of
passion. We may express this worst aspect of
his style by a negation, and say that in its bald-
ness and ugliness it is antipodal to that of
Shakespeare, in whom all graces and all charms,
voices of nature and modulations of art, strength
and breadth of thought and aëry brightness of
fancy are welded together by a full-orbed imagination. Yet this style, abortive only at first
sight, justifies itself like that of the poetry and
in the same way;—by ever trembling on the
brink of that which it is beyond it often to
attain fully; by ever tending upward to a level
at which it may not rest for long. On a closer
scrutiny it discloses qualities only gradually dis-
cerned, like an unsightly garment which in places
blends strangely into a web of richest tissue,
studded here with jewels whose facets gleam,

there breaking as it were into glistening armour. Not only is it continuously sustained by a masculine vigor of thought and pervaded by that unflagging force which itself is a divine afflatus; not only can it produce, by grandly massed passages, a broad and noble effect; not only does its rhetoric deepen often into passion or glow into imaginative beauty or rise to true sublimity, but it now and again gives out surprising, unconscious touches of spontaneous, natural, unstrained emotion; it glides into Shakespearian turns of thought and becomes terse, humorous, discursive, fantastic and various if not subtle; it seems always to suggest more than is disclosed on the surface; it teems with the promise of more than it actually achieves. It is substantially weak but potentially strong.

Connected with this failure of execution in the detail and following from it as a necessary result, is the failure in sense of proportion which leads to incoherency in the whole. These plays have not, any more than the descriptive poems, firm structure or symmetry. Mystery or dramatic poem or historic play, one and all of them are trailing and shapeless, so far as we look in them for articulated parts welded into a perfect whole. We shall presently find Byron professing, and justly, to be influenced by the Greek drama and dominated by a zeal for the unities; but of the Greek spirit he had small perception, and in proportion as he seeks precision and severity of outline his failure is most hopeless and pathetic. The scenes and acts in his painfully elaborated historical plays are not the constituent moments which mark the progress towards the catastrophe, but arbitrary and uneven divisions in an action that hurries or delays at the author's good will.

Passing from the structure to the characterization, we are again met by an old objection. Moving among the persons and accosting each in turn, we are conscious of a sameness in them all. The diversity of the costume serves only to accentuate a common identity—something familiar in the turn of the gestures, however adapted to the rôle they are intended to accompany—a similarity in the mode of utterance, however varied the intonations. The external appearance is that of a multifarious crowd, but the effect rendered by it as a whole is the personality of Byron, as the general murmur that rises from it is his voice. As we look on, our sympathies are compelled to attune themselves to a single strain, strive as they will; our eyes and hearts and minds to perceive all through a single controlling medium, be the scene as varied, the action as changeful as it may.

To complete the bewildering impression which a first perusal of the plays inevitably produces, the fragmentariness of the execution is felt to extend back to the initial conception. From the scattered strokes that make up this dramatic work, we can image forth no rounded outlines of an ordered world, but at best fugitive and one-sided glimpses of a world partially conceived, set down in crude haste by a mind that disdained to revise or re-consider its first disordered judgments. Seen thus far, the dramas are but a subsidiary group among those " swift creations " at which Shelley so marvelled, and if they seem to add a distinct lustre to Byron's poetic galaxy, this is only by an increase of the nebulous multiplicity of its beams.

III.

ALL this may well seem a step backwards; in reality it is the recoil which it is necessary to make *pour mieux sauter*. Byron of all poets is not to be vindicated by slurring over his defects but by enforcing and insisting on them. Only as these are firmly accentuated can they be thrown aside as dross, leaving revealed the pure ore of merit that remains. But the question may still be asked: "Supposing the dross to be purged away, does any of the *dramatist* remain? You say that the main threads of Byron's poetry reproduce themselves in his dramatic work, and that the latter is vitiated by the same faults—in especial the recurrence of the personal motive—as the poetry. Why then did Byron attempt drama at all? Why did he not simply write all these dramatic poems as direct poetry instead of uselessly employing a pseudo-dramatic form?" (i.) To answer this question we must proceed to consider Byron's peculiar dramatic method and principles, and from the clash of his avowed aim with his actual performance, and a comparison of the result with the practice of some other poets, endeavour to strike out a wider principle which shall at once justify his choice of the dramatic form and interpret the nature of the success he achieved in it.

Byron has explained his dramatic principles with sufficient clearness. All that is needed is that we should understand him properly, taking what he means to say, not what he actually says. For here as elsewhere Byron is a child as soon as he begins to reflect. He thinks right, but without knowing it. Did it depend but on him, Duessa could lead him, an easy dupe, but Fidessa is ever at hand to save him by unerring instinct against himself and to turn his very errors into sources of strength. In recording Byron's written opinions I shall con-

(i.) Cf. Note at end.

dense so far as is compatible with clearness, insisting only on the main points.

Speaking generally as to the possibility of producing a great tragedy, Byron says: "I am, however, persuaded that this is not to be done by following the old dramatists, who are full of gross faults, pardoned only for the beauty of their language, but by writing naturally and *regularly*, and producing *regular tragedies* like the *Greeks*; but not in *imitation*—merely the outline of their conduct, adapted to our own time and circumstances, and, of course, *no* chorus." And again: "It appears to me that there is room for a different style of the drama; neither a servile following of the old drama, which is a grossly erroneous one, nor yet *too French*, like those who succeeded the older writers. It appears to me that good English and a severer approach to the rules might combine something not dishonourable to our literature. . . . Whatever faults [*the Doge*] has will arise from deficiency in the conduct rather than in the conception, which is simple and severe."

It is to be noted that his extreme care to attain simplicity in the design and structure of a play (ii.) is not dictated by any reference to its capability for being acted. He declares in reiterated passages that he writes for the reader and the closet, (iii.) not for the stage, of which he has so intense a dislike, (iv.) nor for the audience, whose applauses yield him no pleasure even in prospect (v.). He further explains and emphasizes this statement by the assertion that he does not aim at popularity (vi.) ; and that the sincerity of this repudiation is perfectly genuine; at least so far as the drama is concerned, is proved by yet another doctrine of his, which implies the clearest appre-

(ii.) "The unities, which are my great objects of research."

(iii.) "They might as well act the *Prometheus* of Æschylus [as *Faliero*]. I speak, of course, humbly and with the greatest sense of the distance of time and merit between the two performances, but merely to show the absurdity of the attempt. . . . I write only for the reader."

(iv.) "I have rendered it [*Manfred*] quite impossible for the stage, for which my intercourse with Drury Lane has given me the greatest contempt."

(v.) "The applauses of an audience would give me no pleasure."

(vi.) "You say the *Doge* will not be popular : did I ever write for popularity ? "

ciation of the means by which an ephemeral
popularity was most likely to be evoked (vii.). His
rejection of love as a dramatic motive—a fact as
significant as it is wholly unexpected, and on
which much will be found to turn—is as uncom-
promising as his enforcement of the unities. He
says of it that "unless it is love *furious, criminal*
and hopeless it ought not to make a tragic subject.
When it is melting and maudlin it *does*, but it
ought not to."

Two points, apparently slight but really significant, and making as much against as for the
argument, may still be noticed as further illus-
trating the general principles above enumerated.
The first is that, with all his zeal for the unities,
Byron was no mere theorist, but had a keen

(vii.) "I have also attempted to make a play without love ; and
there are neither rings, nor mistakes, nor starts, nor outrageous
ranting villains, nor melodrame in it. All this will prevent its
popularity."

"As I think that *love* is not the principal passion for tragedy
(and yet most of ours turn upon it), you will not find me a popular
writer."

"*Faliero* was for the closet, not stage ; nothing melodramatic, no
surprises, &c. . . . and no *love*."

perception of the possible limits and capacities of his genius. After finishing *Faliero* he can write : "But many people think my talent *essentially undramatic,* and I am not at all clear that they are not right." And where the question is in regard to a subject not historical, his conviction is still more positive. He will have *Manfred* called "a poem . . . for it is *no drama,* and I do not choose to have it called by so . . . a name." The second point to be noticed confirms this view more fully, and has reference to that quality of mind so eminently characteristic of Byron, which would seem to hamper if not exclude that play of imagination which is the very life-blood of true drama. This was his genuine passion for reality; and at present it will be sufficient merely to advert to the fact without considering its ambiguous testimony to his claims as a dramatist (viii.).

(viii.) Cf. for instance his directions in regard to the notes to *Marino Faliero,* insisting on the strictest accuracy in matters of mere detail.—*Moore's Life,* vol. iv. p. 352.

We are now in a position to extract a pro-
visional meaning from this confusion of rules,
caprices, and common-sense principles, and to
separate what is false in them from what is true.
False, to begin with, were all his mere *rules* and
the idea they were meant to subserve of a formal
drama at once stiff and elaborate and stately.
Byron was as far from being the shaping artist
as the mere playwright.   His construction, if one
may say so, is neither Shakespearian nor *Unitarian.*
False, too, was his disdain of the old drama and
the old dramatists, whose real spirit he misunderstood.   It may be added generally, that in proportion as he follows the letter of his rules he
fails.

What was true—and it completely outweighs
and outbalances the false—was his idea of a new
kind of drama which, however little *Greek,* should
have at least a certain Greek simplicity, and
eschewing all frivolous interests and disdaining
all stage effect and artifice, pursue great or
stirring or noble ideas, using them as themes

through which to set forth the deeper passions,
the yearning aspirations, the baffling problems of
humanity (ix.).

A "new kind of drama" with "Humanity" for
its theme! The man who, with whatever con-
fusions and hesitations could grasp such a
conception as this was not far from being a
dramatic poet; and something more even than
this—the forerunner of a genuine dramatic
reform, reaching back to Shakespeare on the
one hand, reaching forward on the other to new
times, which need ever new methods of expression. That Byron can lay claim to such a
position is as undoubted as that his success
was unconscious.

That critics should have misunderstood and
underrated this success would be beyond comprehension, did we not remember the besetting
sins of criticism—its want of elasticity, its inability
to place itself in a new position or judge correctly

(ix.) Cf. Note at end.

4—2

of the shifting aspect of things, its reluctance to
confess that its mission is to discover and define
before it presumes to judge. This rigidity is
strikingly shown at the present time in reference
to the drama. That we live at the close (if so
much may be hoped) of a non-dramatic literary
era may perhaps explain this dulness of perception, and account for the ambiguity which
has grown up about the term "dramatic." The
gaze of criticism is set eagerly in the direction
of the stage, yet the only spell by which it
deigns to conjure fresh forms is the name of
Shakespeare; and against the bulwark of that
great, misused authority all efforts at reform
seem to beat in vain. It therefore becomes
necessary, in order to explain Byron's position,
to trace the connection between his "new kind
of drama" and the drama called after Shakespeare.
This can be done without temerity, for although
the subject is so great in itself, demanding the
most careful separate treatment, there needs but
to glance at it here, and, traversing it with light-

ning speed, touch merely on the few points required for our comparison.

Starting with the assumption that the sole mission of the dramatic poet is to "hold the mirror up to nature," and that herein is expressed the whole spirit of drama, the question reduces itself to a consideration of the various ways in which this may be done. What was the method of Shakespeare, the type and exemplar of the national-drama at its height? His method is, withdrawn in impartial impersonality, to present the world objectively through *characters*, individually distinct, and developed inevitably, like creations that have been framed by the hand of Nature herself, and yet at the same time interfused on the one hand by broad general traits which link them with humanity at large, on the other with that indefinable distinction, that heroic peculiarity which is the "self" or spirit of the very poet, and without which they would not be Shakespearian.

Next to the Shakespearian or Elizabethan

character-drama, but standing on a lower level, may be placed that inferior but still great drama which represents men with less individuality through certain *types*. Of this kind the best representative is generally allowed to be the French classical drama; and it may be said to be included within the Shakespearian, for Shakespeare's persons are types as well as characters.

Attached to one or other of these forms, or hovering uncertain between the two, modern drama, in its transition from the older to more recent times, has proceeded in always diminishing volume and within an ever-narrowing channel upon a course of steady decline, until it has ceased in every country to be truly national; content where it does not subsist meagrely on the shadow of past glories to reflect what may be roughly epitomized as " society," instead of holding the mirror up to nature, or, as is the case in England more especially, supinely to offer a mere pseudo-dramatic " entertainment," which

is absolutely without. life or substantiality as it
is utterly divorced from any ideal.

The reasons for this inevitable decay will
suggest themselves to many, but can only be
touched on here in so far as they bear reference
to a newer drama which has tended to spring
from the ruins of the old, and which is closely
associated with the name and work of Byron.
To do even thus much is not easy. For this
newer drama, besides being wholly unrecognized
by the inert criticism already referred to, is the
more incapable of being historically traced or
accurately defined in that it has not as yet
passed out of the embryonic stage and is itself
but dimly conscious of its own aims and of its
own future. Its method may however be clearly
enough indicated as resting on *idea* rather than
character. These two elements are not antagonistic
to each other; but as drama is necessarily the
result of their being blended in certain proportions, they involve an antagonism. Hence the
difficulty that confronts the dramatist as to the

exact prominence he shall give on the one hand
to his personages, on the other to the forces of
which they are, after all, but the exponents;
and hence, too, the existence in every drama of
an inherent discord. The difficulty of the adjust-
ment is brought home to us by the consideration
that the sole dramatist who has ever succeeded
on a truly noble and grand scale in exhibiting
the two constituents of drama at equilibrium
was Shakespeare; and even in Shakespeare the
qualities of the playwright, (who would fain
exclude and limit) fall infinitely below the
qualities of the poet, (who would fain comprehend and expand). But since Shakespeare the
discord has gone on increasing, the rift widening
to a chasm as the notion of man the individual
has become overshadowed by all that is included
under the notion of the wider term humanity.
And it is naturally the higher minds, on whom
the vast complexity of modern thought impor-
tunately presses, that have been most conscious
of this truth. Such minds would inevitably be

ed to shun the stage as an arena too narrow and confined for the display of a life which, while it may appear externally to grow poorer and meaner, shows ever more rich and strange and glorious from within. Even the hand of a Shakespeare might seem insufficient to compress within the bounds of individual character emotions that grow more complex as they are handled and thoughts that expand ere they are well grasped. It is at any rate easy to understand how to some few it may have seemed well deliberately to overpass the equilibrium of Shakespeare and, somewhat to enlarge the previous formula, instead of making the idea subservient to the character, make the character subservient to the idea.

An anomalous position, it may be said, since a drama implies action; but literature has never been averse to anomalies when they were the result of a struggle to attain an end felt rather than defined; and that this theory is but the expression of a consistent endeavour to realize the highest conception of drama, as that which mirrors life most largely, directly and vividly, is proved by the fact that it not only lies at the root of the so-called generally weak Literary drama, addressed to an audience of readers, but is the basis of many dramas written professedly for the stage by men whose ideal was wider than the medium they chose for its expression. This may be illustrated by reference to a few great names. The first flutterings of this new spirit may be traced in the dramas of Alfieri. To him, in a present when all life seemed to have died away, there came a breath of the free air of the antique past, and his task henceforth was but to body forth in living fulness the new and glorious ideas with which it inspired him. Later on, Victor Hugo, glowing with youthful passion and stung at heart with pity for the sorrowful human fate, brought to bear upon the solution of the problem the working of a genius too rhetorical yet at once discursive and intense, and in dramas only artificially dramatic illuminated some of the

darker depths of humanity with a radiating though
fitful beam. Among our own later poets, Browning, ranging over the field of human emotion
with largest sympathy and philosophic insight,
interprets in his own language all the motives
that lead to action, while the actors themselves
fade to a vanishing point. And another poet,
equally great though with different powers, and
not deliberately choosing the dramatic form for
his best work, is even more representative.

The actual dramas of our Laureate, in themselves an evidence of his poetic sensitiveness to
the changing ideals of the time, seem to some of
his admirers to be so far failures in that they
indicate on the part of the author rather an
apprehension of the spiritual fact than a full
appreciation of its true nature and bearings. In
reaching back to older models, to which his genius
is unsuited, he wastes, one feels, the strength which
might have gone to the shaping of new ideals.
Hence his so-called dramas partake too much of the
character of studies. They rest on an insubstantial

basis, and herald but dimly a coming era. But
of the era now closing he is the undisputed master,
and its epic dramas are *In Memoriam, The Prin-
cess,* and the *Idylls of the King,* in which the very
nature and individuality of the time are mirrored
in terms of eternal art. Nor should it escape
notice that once at least, in the episode of *Guine-
vere,* where the ruin and anguish of a realm are
personified in the King, the language attains to
a dramatic simplicity of passion and pathos un-
equalled since the older dramatists.

But it was on Germany that, after a long
interval, the true mantle of Shakespeare descended ;
and it is there that we must look for the last
gleams of the old drama which pourtrayed
through great characters, as well as for the birth
of that newer drama, destined hereafter for fresh
triumphs, which, equally great, mirrors large ideas.
Schiller must not be compared with Shakespeare,
but of Schiller's persons it may truly be said, after
all deductions, that they are the only modern
ones who tread the stage touched with a certain

heroic beauty, and stamped with that impress of
reality which fits them to move and act before
a present audience. Nor does it need to recall
that throughout Schiller's dramas there also burns
and breathes a pregnant and lofty *idea*—the idea
of freedom. But a greater, because more comprehensive, poet than Schiller, without being able to
lay claim to Schiller's power of characterization,
in the truest sense continued Shakespeare's work
and is inheritor of Shakespeare's renown. Goethe,
with a profound and comprehensive consciousness
of a universe changed and wider grown since
Shakespeare's day, and with an intellect proportioned to the intricacy of the problem thus
presented, interrogated "Nature" by new methods,
and learnt and communicated her secret. Goethe,
by right of this profound consciousness, this comprehensive vision, is our modern Shakespeare.
His greatness lay partly in perceiving that
whereas the genius of Shakespeare had naturally
evolved heroic figures representative as in a microcosm of the form and pressure of a heroic time,

and typical through it of all humanity, the modern age manifested itself to him who would imaginatively interpret it, as an open secret suggestive of many and complex and potent forces which, by an Æschylean reminiscence, drew the actors along with them in their sweep. Under this conception character is not destroyed, it hardly even loses importance, but it takes spontaneously a new position. A single Shakespearian character will illustrate this. Macbeth, among many others, is a hero who works out a destiny. In Shakespeare the interest of the spectator is centred on Macbeth; with Goethe, treating the same story freely, from the point of view of his own time and his own genius, the attention would have been directed to destiny and withdrawn from Macbeth, the idea expanding as the hero dwindled. The significance of *Faust* seems inexhaustible, but Faust as a personal character becomes more shadowy the more we attempt to grasp him.

Thus the greatness of Shakespeare and the

greatness of Goethe rest on the same basis. They
are supremely great by virtue of that " vision "
which enabled them to hold the mirror up to the
changing idea which we call indifferently Nature
or the Universe or Humanity. Only their methods
necessarily contrast; and to many Goethe chiefly
seems admirable in that, coming after so great
a forerunner, whose ideal he could not hope to
exceed, he was yet able to maintain that ideal
while he retained his originality. And besides
Goethe, Byron, and Byron only, entered into that
charmed circle—unconsciously, led irresistibly by
his genius; but still he entered it, and alone.
The greatness of Byron, however lower in degree,
is the same in kind with that of Shakespeare and
Goethe. He is great by a consciousness like
theirs of a Universe, of Humanity; by the vision
which enabled him, like them, to pierce to the
meaning of it, and by the faculty which, however
imperfect, resembled theirs in its ability to mirror
back in correlative terms of art the impression
thus received. A defective art, it may be said; an

imperfect and erring vision. Granted; but still a vision, and a deeply true and comprehensive one —a vision whose range in his poems is fully acknowledged, but which appears in its full scope, with more eager searchings, with wider workings over the problems of the world and humanity, in his dramas, and his dramas only (ii.).

This, that he had the vision at all, and could render dramatically the impression it gave him, is the primary, the essential fact; that his rendering was touched with a spirit of revolt is secondary, and was an accident of destiny, of circumstance, rather than an inherent necessity of his genius. From the actual struggle of cotemporary life as it unfolded itself Schiller stood aloof; by Goethe, who resumed antiquity, mirrored the age, and foresaw the tendencies of the future it was regarded in that wide and subtle view which included it as part of a larger whole. But Byron Destiny took by the throat and forced into the stress of the time, so that he could not remain

(ii.) Cf. Note at end.

perfectly calm; and lest he should not be wholly the child of his age, but regard it too passionlessly as an artist, embittered his being with the pangs of wounded self-love and personal loss, and convulsed it with the violence of unbridled passions, so that his heart responsive should by the keen anguish within come to a closer corresponden intimacy with the sorrow and darkness without Goethe, in a word, is Olympian, but Byron, in more than mere avowal, in very act, is a Titan and by right of suffering more immediately representative and interesting. His own words on this point must be transcribed here, for they express an axiomatic truth. "The *Prometheus*," he says in one of his letters, "if not exactly in my plan, has always been so much in my head that I can easily conceive its influence over all or anything that I have written."

In the stanza from *Childe Harold* previously quoted, the spirit of the poet was described as driven to take refuge from the world in nature, and as deriving thence the notion of a harmony in

5

which all things have their being. A passage still
more noticeable shows how the same tortured
spirit of self, drawn into an existence wider than
its own, becomes creative:

> " 'Tis to create, and in creating live
>   A being more intense, that we endow
> With form our fancy, gaining as we give
>   The life we image, even as I do now.
> What am I? Nothing: but not so art thou,
>   Soul of my thought! with whom I traverse earth,
> Invisible but gazing, as I glow
>   Mixed with thy spirit, blended with thy birth,
> And feeling still with thee in my crush'd feelings' dearth." (iii.).

*Mixed with thy spirit . . feeling still with thee;
what am I? Nothing; . . gaining as we give
the life we image*—what could better describe the
genesis of dramatic creation? The lacerated soul,
fain of oblivion from its woes or craving intenser
sympathy, lets its fancy play about all the forms
of life, but more artistic than it knows, is fascinated
among the phantoms it evokes and receives back
its inward perturbations on a flood of larger emotion,
of which it had not before dreamed.

(iii.) *Childe Harold*, iii. 6.

We can now define more precisely, though not even yet finally, that "new kind of drama," with Humanity for its theme, towards which Byron was drawn, and differentiating it from the poetry, say that it rested on *great ideas dramatically set forth*; *i.e.* set forth in relation to humanity. What the nature of these ideas more especially was, and what their limits, will be discussed further on; at present it is enough to take the definition as it stands and apply it as an elucidating principle to the apparent contradictions of the Byronic dramas. As regards plot, action and delineation of character, they may be defective, but where the idea possesses him, Byron never fails to dramatize it; and what is far more, his dramatization will be found to be always appropriate as well as complete, and characterized by what is, in the noblest sense, invention and a shaping imagination. He is devoid of consummate dramatic style, but at his best—that is, when he faithfully follows the idea—his style takes on that "inevitableness," or, in other words, that "absolute sincerity and strength" which are the mark of the

greatest poetry, distinguishing it absolutely from
mere verse or the product of even high literary
skill—a strength that comes solely from the insight
of genius, and that is imperfect only as genius itself
is human and imperfect. On this principle, too, the
actors become fully adequate. For if not singly
dramatic, they produce the requisite dramatic effect
by groups, each contributing in due subordination
and degree to the broad developement of the
motive idea. Nor, under this view, is it a great
matter that the stimulating idea starts so often, in
the first instance, from the personality of the poet—
that Byron, Prometheus-like, is the protagonist,
the utterer of his own grief; if in the long pauses
he make real to Io, type of knowledge-seeking man,
the long tale of mortal error, and all that was before,
and all that shall be after; if too, like Prometheus,
from his tortured eminence he can survey not only
the earth beneath but the heavens above, make
immortals speak with mortal tongues, and by the
enchantment of his personality charm within ken
divine denizens of the air.

Intoxicated, as it were, by the great ideas that possessed him, haunted by that riddle of humanity which his inward suffering enabled him to feel so keenly, but the full solution of which he felt to be beyond his grasp, it is easy to perceive that Byron, whatever his conscious principles, could only be swayed violently in certain directions, and impetuously reject all minor interests and emotions that did not minister to the one overwhelming dramatic idea that for the time entranced his mind. He could not stoop and dally to accommodate persons to the stage when he had the tragedy of mankind before his eyes; he could hardly even find patience to draw individual types when the larger issues of human fate demanded his whole utterance effectually to express them. Humanity seeking and hoping but baffled; humanity stirred by religious yearnings, racked by philosophic doubts; humanity in mid-stress of emotion, battling against eternal problems —how could one whom such themes carried out of himself stoop to palter with sentimental intrigues or delineate the gradual phases of individual passion?

This—and no want of dramatic aptitude, is the true explanation of Byron's aversion for the stage, of his passion for simplicity, of his total rejection of love as a dramatic motive unless it be " furious and criminal," *i.e.* unless it form an integral part of the larger passion of humanity.   This will also be found to explain his comparative failure in the historical plays, which by their very nature demand a freer Shakespearian variety and play of character

A certain heroic simplicity, a largeness and one-ness of note, are the natural outcome of the springs that impelled Byron's dramatic energy and that constitute its essential strength.   This law it will be my endeavour to disentangle and clearly set forth in each of the extant dramas ; but it also receives remarkable illustration and confirmation from certain subjects which Byron had the intention of treating dramatically, as well as from certain others which were his avowed favourites in early youth.   These, at the risk of anticipating a little, it will be worth while to examine, for the subjects of a poet's predilection are the revelations of his genius, the direction of which it should be possible, on a correct theory, to deduce from them. In this case, moreover, the examination will lead up to an enunciation of our final definition of the Byronic drama.

Taking indiscriminately the subjects which Byron had it in his mind to dramatize and the plays which he tells us captivated his youthful imagination, we find among the former *Francesca of Rimini* and *Tiberius* (iv.); among the latter, the *Prometheus* and *Seven against Thebes* of Æschylus and the *Medea* of Euripides (v.). Of the *Prometheus* I have already spoken, but it cannot be too often insisted on that *Prometheus* is the very type of the Byronic protagonist—the agonized utterer of his own woes first, but through them the interpreter to men of their mortal fate; a voice whose lamen-

(iv.) " Pondered the subjects of four tragedies . . . *Sardanapalus* . . *Cain* . . *Francesca of Rimini* . . and I am not sure that I would not try *Tiberius.*"—*Byron's Diary.*

(v.) "Of the *Prometheus* of Æschylus I was passionately fond as a boy (it was one of the Greek plays we read thrice a year at Harrow) ; indeed, that and the *Medea* were the only ones except the *Seven* which ever much pleased me."—*Byron's Letters.*

tations take gradually wider compass, defiant, as
before a doom which seems only dark, but not
without a chastening intimation of hope.   And the
Prometheus includes the *Seven*, as the greater the
less; for in the latter play what attracted Byron
was doubtless the inflexible haughtiness of Eteocles.
The *Medea* and *Francesca* come under a different
category and reflect as clearly another aspect of the
Byronic idea.   Medea is a very individual figure,
but the moral of her passion has more than individual significance.   It shatters domestic peace,
ruins families, and in its far-reaching consequences
may embroil states.   It is a factor of disturbance
in the chaos of a world out of joint.   From somewhat the same general point of view would Byron
have approached the subject of *Francesca*, and it
is needless to say with what terrible effect the
passion, the ruin and the pathos of the story
would have started into life beneath his hand; but
he would also by masterly, subtle and inevitable
touches have differentiated this story of passion
from all other stories of passion, and beyond this,

by unerring application of the same principle, differentiated *Francesca*, the victim of passion, from all similar victims, by a strain of peculiar tenderness and pathos personal to that pitiable heroine. For, in the extant plays, women play an important part, and beneath an apparent similarity display a perfect dramatic individuality and infinite gradations of character.

But *Tiberius* is by far the most interesting of those subjects in which a legitimate critical anticipation may seek suggestions of character-istics afterwards to be confirmed by reference to the actual plays. Byron instinctively sees in it a field for "*his* tragic;" (vi.) and what foremost strikes us in his words is the distinctness of ideal, the saneness and reasonableness of method which they imply. The admirable sanity that underlay

---

(vi.) " I think that I could extract a something, of *my* tragic at least, out of the gloomy sequestration and old age of the tyrant . . . by softening the *details*, and exhibiting the despair which must have led to those very vicious pleasures. For none but a powerful and gloomy mind overthrown would have had recourse to such solitary horrors, being also at the same time *old* and the master of the world."—*Byron's Diary.*

the surface irregularities of Byron's genius here
betrays its presence artistically, softening a theme
that might have seemed to be chosen only for
its congenial horror. Far from flinging himself
carelessly into the horror, Byron sees clearly the
necessity of moderating it, of moulding and
developing it dramatically. But still more interesting than in its suggestion of dramatic
design is this rough outline of an unwritten play
in its complete foreshadowing of the moral motive
or intention which lay as the fundamental inspiration at the heart of the Byronic drama. The
more prominent features in the portraiture of the
Byronic Tiberius it is easy enough to forecast.
At his first appearance on his lonely rock, the
gloomy and sequestered tyrant would have been
painted for us with something of Promethean
aloofness and agony—a wreck of empire, yet re-
taining traces of his former majesty; aged and
an abandoned votary of hideous pleasures, yet
breathing unutterable hatred, scorn and defiance
against the vile world he has quitted. And as

the action developed, the lights and shadows of the character would have been heightened as none other than Byron could heighten them, and all the traits of that monstrous and diseased mind—its raging lust, its dark and savage brutality, its concentrated despair, its fitful gleams of half-mad cunning or hypocrisy—would have been laid bare to our view, emerging at intervals beneath the appearances of ghastly merriment and unreal revelry. And at this picture of mere blinding despair, acknowledging its marvellous force, but assuming it to be the exaggerated delineation of the poet's own personality, the popular criticism of Byron would stop dead, believing him capable of no more. But Byron's own words, taken in conjunction with his actual work, enable us to infer that he was capable of much more, and that his mind was too great, too human, too *dramatic* to rest in the negation of despair. For the picture of Tiberius, in Byron's emphatic words, is that of a powerful mind *overthrown*, and the very depth of that *despair which*

must have led to those very vicious pleasures, is
but the reaction from the hope, the yearning, the
aspiration which Byron's true dramatic instinct
foresaw in the tyrant's early career.

We have, then, two modifications to add to the
Byronic portraiture of Tiberius as likely to be
conceived by the popular judgment. First,
though we cannot tell the exact method, Byron
would have shown the silver side of this tissue of
horrors, and by exhibiting the effect in the light
of its cause, mitigated the horror to pathos,
heightened the ethical effect, and left the mind
of the spectator purged through pity. Secondly,
as in the *Francesca*—for Byron's heroes have as
distinct an individuality as his heroines—the poet
would have made all the threads of the tragic
passion centre in the very nature of Tiberius
himself, so as to render him, not by accumulation
of external accidents, but by reason of essential
identity of character, individual and distinct from
all other Byronic protagonists.

All this may seem fanciful enough, but is

really based on sober inference and is full of
value for our inquiry.   For Tiberius, though not
an exaggerated Byron, reflects most clearly an
ethical tendency that strongly marked the genius
of Byron, suggesting the possession by him of
that larger element of hope or belief in good,
without which a great poet, still less a great
dramatist, can hardly be supposed possible.   It is
necessary emphatically to show that in contemplating the riddle of the painful earth, Byron's
denunciation is but the measure of his aspiration,
and that although for him the solution was and
could not but be impossible, it hovered always
before his mind as a haunting possibility (vii.).
The presence in Byron's work of this larger note
of hope needs the more to be insisted on as
criticism has seemed so resolutely to ignore or
leave it out of sight, and it supplies all that is
requisite to complete our definition of Byron's

(vii.) Cf. a remarkable entry in his diary on *Hope*, beginning :
" Why at the very height of desire," &c.—*Moore's Life*, vol. v.
page 89.

dramatic principles, to show what were the limitations of a poetic insight at once wide and piercing, and to point out how those limitations applied to the general ideas under which he treated humanity as a dramatist.

In giving the complete definition it is needful to revert to those two characteristic strains which were discovered to run through the poetry. These were the note of Revolt, expressive of defiance and despair, and the note of Humanity, expressive of aspiration and hope. And blending with these dual strains, affecting but not affected by them, was the note of Nature, expressive of a calm impartial, almost immoral, but beneficent in operation.

These dual tendencies take shape and personality in the dramas as a Dipsychus, working through many characters and interchanging among them, but ever clearly to be perceived. Sometimes the aspiration which tends to the good, and the bitterness which springs from the rejection or despair of it, are blended in a single protagonist, as it were a Byron who acts and suffers; but the personal motives of hope or despair are so skilfully enhanced and deepened in the persons of the minor actors, and so made to merge in the wider issues of destiny, that true dramatic proportion is never lost. More rarely the opposing principles are embodied with somewhat more distinctness in separate characters (viii.). But, however assigned or distributed, the characters of the Byronic drama—undramatic only in form, fully dramatic in spirit—resolve themselves into these two: the soul that, while it suffers and feels loss, is capable of hope and love; and the soul that, while it renounces, would draw all others down to its own bitterness. And always accompanying these two, as a moral necessity of their existence, and rather a part of the very texture of fate than an actor in it, is that pathetic and much misunderstood character, the Byronic woman, who, in her weakness, a toy between the opposing principles of good and evil embodied in the

(viii.) As in the *Deformed Transformed.*

actors, completes with these the human tragedy, suffering where they enjoy and bearing while they act. And, given actors of such a type, Nature, which seems so intrusive in a drama, is not superfluous, having a twofold purpose; for she is, first, the vasty background on which the puppets must play out their petty parts; and, secondly, that broad haven of repose wherein from time to time Dipsychus must find rest or distraction—even as Faust goes off to the Brocken. And in speaking of *Faust* it is impossible to avoid noting parenthetically how closely Goethe's and Byron's methods touch, and what a strong confirmation of the latter's power is afforded by the unconscious similarity. For although we must not confine Byron's Dipsychus within the Faust circle, nor attempt to press the analogy between the two, the Faust motive does, in its world sweep, in some sense include the Byronic ideal within its circumference. For the nobler half of Byron's Dipsychus is ever prone to go forth seeking for knowledge or thirsting to enjoy; and the worser half not only touches with Mephistopheles at many points, but in the *Deformed Transformed*—though here, perhaps, with some conscious imitation—actually blends with him. Nor is Gretchen without her analogue, seeing that she must appear, the same in suffering as she is changeful by circumstance, in every Byronic play. But it would be fanciful to pursue the analogy. It signifies merely that Byron too trod the human stage and entered into the secrets of the human heart.

The complete formula of Byron's dramatic method may now be given thus: Its aim is the exhibition in successive dramas of some grand phase or aspect of Humanity acting out as Dipsychus its destiny under stress of the conflicting impulses of good and evil within it and without. The hypothesis remains to be enforced, but assuming it for the moment as proved, its significance deserves to be noticed. It has both a direct and indirect value. In the first place it bridges the interval between poetry and drama.

For in naming the Byronic protagonist "Dipsychus," it is implied that the field of description
has been left for that of action; that all the
dramatic elements that lay dormant in the poetry
- the glow, the passion, the satiric humour, the
fiery energy—have become as it were embodied,
and that Byron as dramatist, instead of merely
contemplating from afar, traverses, explores, and
displays through action many spheres of human
emotion. Secondly, the possession of a motive
idea, however it may be objected to as cramping
and confining artistic freedom, is at least a powerful instrument in the artist's hands. To take a
truism and illustrate it by platitudes ends in
mere sterility. But an idea is a product of
genius, is never sterile, and implies a possibility
of developement answering to reserves of power
in the mind that produced it. A consideration
of what this power was in Byron's case will lead
us to a final estimate of his genius, and afford
the means of bringing to a conclusive test the
cardinal points on which it has been impugned.

Meanwhile the theory itself, the method through which that genius was more immediately manifested, demands to be lifted from the sphere of assertion into that of proof. And this can only be done by tracing in each of the extant dramas the leading motive or idea on which it rests, disentangled from all that is non-essential to its comprehension.

IV.

IN treating of Byron's dramatic ideal it is
needful to guard against two misconceptions. It
must be distinctly regarded, not as a rigid rule
but as an animating principle, formulated
only for convenience sake, and merely implying,
beyond an element common to all drama, the
particular type which his genius tended to assimi-
late. It is a key that will serve to unlock and
explain all the dramas, but it must sometimes
be applied in the spirit, not in the strict letter.
Secondly, it might be urged as a valid objection
that the principle thus laid down is opposed to,
if it does not flatly contradict, Byron's own
avowed principle. Now Byron as a critic need
not disturb our peace, but it may be well to
glance at this point in passing, as well because
it needs to be clearly understood as that it
affords an invaluable criterion for estimating the

unconscious working of Byron's genius and vindicating it against itself.

It is certain that every poetic nature includes within itself a critical element, and it may be that the inmost secret of criticism lies open to the great poet alone. But it is equally certain that the highest poetic genius, though ever essentially linked in a most subtle relation with critical appreciativeness, may exist in its perfection while the sister faculty is dormant, or atrophied, or misdeveloped by force of circumstances. So it was with Carlyle, whose true "poetic" message we so blindly confused with his invective; so it is with some writers yet living, in whom posterity will have to search for the true instinct beneath the outrageous expression; so it was transcendently with Byron. No sane judge would look in Byron for the critical judgment in perfect counterpoise with the poetic sway; but the same judge would most eagerly seek to penetrate through those outward extravagances to the core of the true poetic genius underlying them, and

to the *flashes* of critical insight which this would
pre-suppose. Byron's spirit we shall find not with
the poets of the eighteenth century, not with
the vain pursuers of dramatic unities, but in a
very different sphere. Yet the former were just
those fields where the letter of his criticism
could expatiate. His method is easy to grasp.
His true critical instinct seizes on some weak
place in the armour of his foes, as, for instance,
their depreciation of Pope, and, precipitating itself
upon that, to the exclusion of weightier relations,
is further goaded and incensed by opposition to
heap paradox upon paradox, while the innate
workings of the poet's own impetuous thought
come in with misapplied creative force to complicate the appreciation and imbue it with the
last strain of incongruous confusion. In the same
way he has only to identify the genius of poets
to whom he is ostensibly antagonistic but really
akin with what seems to him their laxity of
method, in order to rush at once to principles
at the opposite extreme to theirs. Byron, in

short, as a critic, is like a man tracing with his staff vague figures on the sand, while his eye and thought are ranging over distant horizons (i.).

Happily, apart from all abstract considerations, we can point to an analogous instance of a poet-critic which will be admitted by all. Wordsworth constantly confounded the true poetic simplicity of diction with mere vulgarity of diction, and won success by a splendid disregard of his own theory. Byron's similar insistence on his historical plays as the outcome of his dramatic theory, enforced as it is by the apparent acquiescence of his critics, has had some part in diverting atten-

(i.) Many illustrations might be given were the subject to be treated at length; but two crucial instances must suffice—Byron's depreciation of Shakespeare and his appreciation of Goethe. In the former case it is enough to ask the reader who has any sense of humour to observe the poet's true critical instinct, stimulated by passing stings of vanity, and angered by stupid opposition, fastening upon what is superficially defective in its great object. The latter instance is far more important, and has a special bearing on our subject. For here we see Byron's spirit, unhampered by accidental prepossessions, piercing through the husks of an unfamiliar language to what is spiritually greatest in the time and most akin to itself. For, as will be brought out more fully later on, Goethe and Byron are at least akin in this, that both exhibit the ideal in special relation to their cotemporary present.

tion from the true worth and proportion of his
dramatic work as a whole; and merely to exhibit
this in a single view is already a long step in
the direction of our right appreciation of him as
a dramatist.

Disregarding, then, exclusive technical distinctions, we find Byron's dramatic work to consist of
a group of eight dramas and dramatic poems;
and these again, looking only to the internal
significance of each piece and not the order of
its production in time, fall easily into three
divisions. The first, consisting of *Manfred*, *Cain*,
and *Heaven and Earth*, forms a trilogy; the
second comprises the *Deformed Transformed* and
Sardanapalus; the third, the historical plays and
Werner.

Throughout the first group the dramatic interest
centres exclusively in the idea; that is, we seem
conscious only of certain fatal forces working their
way blindly to issues of good and evil through
human agents. These agents are: the protagonist,
whose force and originality fit him to be the

direct instrument of destiny; the woman, who from her nature enters into the action only indirectly and in close reference to the man; the subsidiary characters, who serve to complete the action in their degree; and the choruses which, as impersonal dramatic voices, aid with large and broad dramatic effect. Moreover, the idea as it developes creates its own imaginative atmosphere, into which nature largely enters, and gathers about itself its appropriate body of philosophy or thought.

The trilogy is a representation of human fate under three ascending phases, which are successively delineated through the three protagonists Manfred, Cain, and Japhet. Its course thus proceeds by a continuous developement of the idea, the ethical import increasing as the conception expands. It leads us from the individual up to humanity as a whole, and beginning on a note of personal revolt, ends with the despair of a world undone. At the same time this revolt suggests a hope as large and an aspiration as impassioned, which it contains by implication, and from which it is a natural revulsion.

Manfred is the author's *Hamlet*—the attempted solution of life's riddle by a soul weaker than Hamlet's own. Byron here enacts Dipsychus, and forgets himself in the part. A husk of vulgar melodrama enshrouds the play, hiding a finer kernel of truth. To this husk belong the flippant and careless imitation of Goethe in the picture of Manfred the dabbler in magic and theatric evoker of spirits; the general design that would fain cheat us into terror and pity by a mechanical mystery, and the melodramatic parade of diseased emotion.

But to all this there is a finer dramatic and imaginative side. The interest of Manfred lies not in the suspense of his fate—which is assured by his errors—but in the conflict between good and evil in a soul above the "common order," and in the tragic pity of the spectacle. Manfred is the Byronic hero in his crudest form. As contrasted with Cain, Arnold, Sardanapalus, his peculiarity is to be <u>a man not of one clear ideal</u>, <u>but of many confused ones</u> (ii.). He would know all and enjoy all. "His knowledge and his powers and his will," his aspirations and his passions lift him above the ordinary herd to whom a heaven or a hell were alike impossible; but he is no mere voluptuary, and it is only lack of some "wiser mingling" of its glorious elements that leaves his mind a chaos of unregulated impulses and bears the scale down on the side of evil. Then what was his strength becomes his weakness; so that he who had "a mind to comprehend the universe" has become a thing that all might pity; and even the pride with which he faces destiny is but the haughty confession of his inability to guide his life aright. In this weakness and the torturing contrast it implies lies his dramatic force. His sufferings, like his aspirations, are of "an immortal nature." He is what he is, yet "should have been a noble creature;"

(ii.) Cf. Speech of the First Destiny: "Hence! avaunt! he's mine," &c.—Act ii. Scene 4.

his satiated soul is o'er-wearied and sick unto
death, yet "in its youth," ere yet it was "averse
from life," had "earthly visions and noble aspirations." So, ceasing to act and moralizing Hamlet-
like (iii.) on the enigma of destiny, he drifts to
darkness. Again, the poignancy of his despair
gives a fine edge to his imagination. A sense
of the solace and refreshment that are in Nature
fills his mind more exquisitely as the possibility
of their attainment becomes less, and makes him
clairvoyant of her inmost mystery. He would
fain be "The viewless spirit of a lovely sound, A
living voice, a breathing harmony, A bodiless en-
joyment." Ecstacy so fine must be creative; and
accordingly it takes shape, partially in those spirits
which "compass earth about and dwell In subtler
essence," completely in the Witch of the Alps, a
fay embodied of all that can charm in mortality
but compounded "in an essence of purer elements."

(iii.) Cf. the Shakespearian passages :
   "The mind which is immortal," &c.—Act iii. Scene 4.
   "How beautiful is all this visible world," &c.—Act i. Scene 2.
   "We are the fools of time and terror," &c.—Act ii. Scene 2.

Manfred does not fall alone. His destruction has involved that of Astarte, who is but another side of his being; for her pangs are only the translation into sufferance of his passion, as her perplexed and visionary fate is nothing else than the reflex of his tumultuous and erring existence.

This drama must be read in the light of its close. The struggle was only hard while it lasted. That over, it is not "so difficult to die;" and with death comes clearness and returning magnanimity and remorse. The dying speech of Manfred throws back a softening touch over the jarring errors of the past, darkly foreshadows a larger hope, and ends the drama on a note of reconciliation.

If Manfred was Byron and something more, Cain is a conception infinitely higher and opens immeasurable horizons. Manfred, as a Hamlet-like soul, is interesting to men, but Cain is the race itself, and his ruin the ruin of mankind. The poem is at once the mythus of the human mind that "looks before and after;" the tragedy of its aspiration that thirsts vainly for an apprehended good; the drama of its Paradise Re-lost. Dipsychus is here distributed between Cain and Lucifer. Cain as a mere incarnation of revolt is inexplicable and undramatic. But his revolt is the measure of his aspiration, and thus becomes clear and explicable and grandly dramatic (iv.). Sympathy is the ground-work of his character; human affection pulses in him at full. To his parents he is not undutiful; to his brothers and sisters he can say, crossed as he is, " Your gentleness must not be harshly met." He is " wrought upon " by " Abel's earnest prayer." For Adah his love is such that " rather than see her weep " he would " bear all; " and the sight of his son Enoch awakes in him an inexhaustible tenderness (v.). Akin to his human sympathy is his intellectual aspiration, which seeks indeed knowledge, but only as being " the road to happiness." Nor will he believe

---

(iv.) Byron has, in this instance, clearly expressed his dramatic purpose. The despair and consequent murder arise, he explains, from Cain's " rage and fury against the inadequacy of his state and his conceptions."

(v.) Act iii. Scene i.

that evil must ever be a part of all things, for his own emphatic avowal is: *"I thirst for good."* The beginnings of the tragedy are by now apparent, but there is still hope. Cain's "mind of large discourse" apprehends an injustice in his fate, but may' not a larger knowledge solve it? He would only be assured that all is not in vain. "A thousand swelling thoughts, a thousand fears" are within him; "knowledge" is his reiterated cry (vi.). At this point he meets Lucifer, who is but his complement—a Cain superhuman and immortal. His revolt begins where Cain's leaves off, and is based on defiant *hopelessness.* Byron, therefore, with perfect consistency represents him as capable of sympathizing with Cain, but unfeelingly, and as showing involuntary reminiscent touches of magnanimity and pity—the insidious traits of a spirit which by the very nature of its being seeks to involve others in its loss. Against

(vi.)   "Thou canst not
Speak aught of knowledge which I would not know
And do not thirst to know, and bear a mind
To know."—Act i. Scene i.

this hopelessness clashes Cain's yet unquenched
hope, and the tragedy is consummated. Cain is
what he is. Were he weaker it were his salvation.
But he cannot "think and endure" supinely as
the fiend mockingly advises him. *Thinking*, he
must hope, and, the hope destroyed, revolt. Aspiration, turned back on itself, creates an eddying
madness in his brain, and he slays—not Abel, but
injustice momentarily personified. The deed done,
his human affections surge back; he feels horror,
remorse, and would willingly give his own life for
the brother he has loved and slain.

To Cain is given his counterpart Adah—the
woman who feels and loves as fulfilment of the
man who aspires and would know. The boundless desire of Cain is outbalanced by the noble
comprehensiveness of her love and sympathy.
" Who," she exclaims, " could be happy and
alone, or good ? " Alone, she " could not nor
would be happy." This unselfishness comes out in
the tears she sheds for Lucifer, whom she mistrusts,
and in the swift apostrophe when her parents are

mentioned: " Would I could die for them so they might live." And how much wiser is her feeling than Cain's reasoning! Hers is no un-reflecting love. Its note is clear-sightedness. It reasons, and therefore wisely will not reason. She cannot answer the " immortal thing " who yet, she feels, " steps between heart and heart," but, steadfast to her intentions, urges Cain to " choose love." Nor does her devotion blind her for a moment. Cain she would never leave though his God left him ; yet while she clings to the murderer, shrinks from the deed that calls for her self-sacrifice. Nor, at the last, is she a mere clinging Medora, but a resolved woman. Henceforth her office is " to dry up tears and not to shed them ; " and her last words have almost the sternness of an exhortation : " Now, Cain, I will *divide thy burden* with thee."

The idea of *Cain*, involving as it does the problem of man's being, demands to be shown in its relation to human lives in general. Hence the dramatization, which is effected by a small but adequate group of subsidiary characters. Abel and Zillah, in dramatic contrast to Cain and Adah, suggest the tranquillity of the life that is at one with itself. The deed of Cain dissipates this tranquillity and at once lets loose the anarchic discords it had but filmed. The remorse of the murderer himself, the sad resignation of Adam, the mute despair of Zillah, the crowning denunciation of Eve, attest, in an overwhelming climax, the complete disintegration of the human ideal; and the tremendous "*But with me!*" of Cain expresses not merely the burden of his own punishment but the burden of the mystery of the human spirit ever distracted between its aspiration and its destiny.

This drama moves in an atmosphere finely reflective of its spiritual meaning. It is a drama of the yearning intellect, and the starry world of space is opened as if to afford room for the spirit's utmost expansion (vii.); it is a drama of human relations, and the sway of the heart's

(vii.) Act ii. Scene I.

emotion finds an outlet in reiterated passages of tenderness and beauty (viii.); it is a drama of loss, and yearning cadences as for some " regretted Eden " continually sigh through it like the moanings of an Æolian harp (ix.).

Heaven and Earth, the third member of the trilogy, presents the final consummation of the world-drama; the death-hour of

> ———— " The abhorred race
> Which could not keep in Eden their high place,
>   But listened to the voice
> Of knowledge without power."

In *Cain* there were necessarily human actors. In this drama the subject is the doom of Earth herself, the universal mother, and the actors are but the voices that express her throes.

This world-doom is concentrated and connected with humanity in the person of Japhet, who, with the Earth-spirits, plays Dipsychus. The cer-

(viii.) Cf. as above, Act iii. Scene 1 ; and " My sister Adah," &c., Act. ii. Scene 2.

(ix.) Cf. Cain's speech : " I have looked out," &c., Act i. Scene 1, and Adah's speech :

> " Oh my mother, thou . . .
> But we thy children ignorant of Eden," &c., *Ibid.*

tainty of the catastrophe is reflected in the irre-
mediableness of his sorrow, which is brooding,
meditative and unrelieved by hope.   It is also enhanced by being unshared.   For Japhet's love is
rejected and becomes itself "but sorrow."   Yet
this surging sea of love and sorrow issues in no
personal wail, but in a yearning passion of pity
over men, his "fellow-beings," his "kinsmen"—a
pity touched with some sense of the injustice of
their fate (i.).   This jarring note is taken up by
the Earth-spirits, and changed into a pæan of evil
triumphant over the older mortal race and to be
perpetuated in the new.   Still, over this moral
desolation, though enhancing rather than reliev-
ing it, there hovers a broken gleam of hope, an
intimation dimly perceived by Japhet of a time
of redemption, when

> " The eternal will
> Shall deign to expound this dream
> Of good and evil." (ii.)

(i.) Cf. Japhet's opening soliloquy in Part I. Scene 3.

(ii.) This drama was never completed, and so remains Byron's
Prometheus Bound.   But the poet expressly tells us he intended to
continue it by "a way he had in view."   Though we can only

To this world-dirge the lesser actors are contributory voices speaking from the vasty background of Nature in which they are absorbed. Aholibamah and Anah seem living enough, and are links of human interest. The former, a true descendant of Cain, would dare for her lover " an immortality of agonies; " and the spirit of Abel re-lives in Anah, than whom " more loving dust ne'er wept beneath the skies." But their temperaments merely suggest the manner in which each will confront the darkly dubious fate into which they are shortly to be withdrawn by their angel lovers. And these angel lovers themselves are hardly more than notes swelling the chorus of doom, a part in which is taken by the archangel Raphael.

The dramatic presentment of the subject is perfect. Borne forward on a rugged but effective

---

speculate on the result, it is deeply interesting to think that this Second Part might have proved Byron's *Prometheus Unbound*, his drama—on a larger scale than *Sardanapalus*—of Reconciliation. In that case we should have had an actual manifestation of that higher side of Byron's genius, which now we can only infer.

stream of versification, this drama of world-sorrow
sweeps on, as with the confused sound of many
voices, through prelude and progress to its close.
The dread hush of nature at the beginning accords with the " calm of desolation " in Japhet's
mind, the " ominous fears " of Anah, the vati-
cinations of Noah. The rushing sound and
laughter of the Earth-spirits announces the first
stir of " approaching chaos," the nearness of
which is also foreboded in the agitated converse
of mortals and angels. The deluge is the outward symbol of the consummated woe. As the ark
floats over the rising waters, the desolation without is felt to be as nothing to the overwhelming
sorrow within the breast of Japhet, and an effect
is produced on the mind such as springs from a
power akin to that which created *Lear*.

Throughout this trilogy, nature, as the background and external scene, plays an emphatic
part, intensifying and reflecting the action.
Manfred paints the perturbations of an individual
soul. Accordingly the scene is ordinary nature,

but nature seen in her grandest and most terrible aspects.   In *Cain* the issues of man's destiny are to be worked out, and the background is proportioned to the awfulness of the problem. Nature here appears as the material cosmos. From a larger and primeval earth we are borne upwards among starry worlds, gain glimpses of Heaven and descend to the abodes of Hades.   In the doom-drama of *Heaven and Earth* the scenery is as a world personified, a world in throes, a world suffering like a Titaness—a conception of huge gloom, sorrow and catastrophal disaster.

The two dramas comprising the second group move, unlike individually, in a sphere of their own, more human than that of the trilogy, more imaginative than that of the historical plays. The developement of the idea is still the paramount motive, but this idea, by its very nature, involves increased dramatic play and increased developement of character, the former being chiefly noticeable in the *Deformed Trans-formed*, the latter in *Sardanapalus*. The pro-

tagonist, the heroine, and in their degree the
subsidiary characters assume more strongly marked
individual traits, while the choric parts dwindle
proportionately in importance.   Correspondingly
the imaginative conception becomes less grandi-
ose and less dependent on nature, but gains a
wider ethical range; while the philosophy or
thought is more deeply human and meditative.

The *Deformed Transformed* is only a fragment,
but a precious one.   It is peculiarly Byronic, the
idea being as clear and as dramatically evolved
as the structural plan is weak and incoherently
developed.   Here for once Byron presents Dipsychus, self and other-self, in definite twy-natured
form, and while directly imitating Goethe, (iii.).
retains his originality.   The drama, compared to
Faust, is as world-glimpse to world-view, but the
glimpse is of piercing and comprehensive effect.
The trilogy had dealt with the problems of
man's being and destiny; this drama treats of

(iii.) Cf. as a slight and therefore significant instance of this
imitation, the episode of the black steeds, Part i. end of Scene I.

man under a more distinctively human aspect, as
the noblest production of nature, as the glorious
creature full of all mundane capabilities, a being
complete in himself, a divinity in mortality. Its
theme is earthly grandeurs and glories and the
nullity of them—"immortal men and their great
motives."

The environment of this play breathes an appropriate atmosphere of greatness. A kind of
flashing, antique beauty pervades it. The grand
note is first struck in the passing of the Phantoms (iv.); the main stage is nothing less than
antique Rome itself; the characters are of noble
rank and have the inward stamp of nobility.

The Dipsychus who treads this scene is a bril-
liant conception. Arnold, the protagonist, is a
Faust inspired of the antique spirit. Cæsar, his
other-self, is a Mephistopheles, whose levity and
malevolence are tinged with a peculiar Byronic
bitterness. The characterization begins on an emphatic note. Arnold is at first but the "angel-

(iv.) Part, i. Scene I.

spirit" in a deformed body, and has endured all
the pangs of that discord ere he attains to the
union of a perfect spirit and a perfect body in
the appropriate personality of Achilles. Hence
the harmony when attained is felt with a rapturous
fulness of reality that breaks out in the exclamation : " I love and I shall be beloved! Oh life!
At last I feel thee! Glorious spirit!" (v.) In
the utterance of these words he has found his
ideal; and what that ideal is should be carefully
noticed. It is no mere sordid ambition, no vague
or haunting desire. It is simply the expansion of
the " glorious spirit " within him in every direction of noble activity. He is an Achilles " brave
as beauteous," " generous as lovely ;" and it is as an
Achilles that he loves and aspires. All is now
prepared for the tragic conflict between this soul
of boundless aspiration and sympathy and its
other haunting self, the antithesis of all to which
it aspires. Arnold's natural desire is for action;
he would be errant " where the world is thickest "

that he may "behold it in its workings;" and straightway comes back the mocking answer: "That's to say where there is war And woman in activity." Later, when he begins to feel the failure of mere action to satisfy the want within him, and would fain be "at peace—in peace," he is assured by Cæsar that "*commotion* is the extremest point of life." The sight of Rome calls up to his mind the thought of all that is great and noble in humanity, but only to mock it with the after-thought of the Nemesis of ruin and degradation that awaits the doomed city. At the least, he would fain show himself "a man;" and what men really are is implied in Cæsar's unanswerable retort, "Thou feelest and thou seest" (vi.)—an argument that appeals with all the more cogency to the latent despondency within Arnold from the sight of Cæsar himself, ever by him and wearing his old hunchback form. And the moral of the whole drama as far as it goes is summed up in the fearful irony

(vi.) Part ii. Scene 2.

of Cæsar's soliloquy: "This is the consequence of giving matter The power of thought" (vii.).

The Gretchen of the piece and the complement of Arnold's better part is Olimpia. She is noble both in rank and character, as befits the probable mate of Arnold, but doomed, we feel, to be lowly enough in the sufferings fate holds in store for her. Though but lightly sketched, she is revealed to us as a definite creation. The effect of her peculiar beauty and nobility is rendered, by a Shakespearian touch, through the impression it produces on others. Arnold says: "Alive or dead, thou essence of all beauty, I love but thee;" and even Cæsar is constrained to exclaim: "The beautiful half-clay and nearly spirit! I am almost enamoured of her."

Just as finely is Arnold's nature, on its more virile side, reflected and emphasized in the character of Bourbon, whose magnanimity appears in his reflections on the approaching downfall of Rome. The other characters are slight, but

(vii.) Cf. the whole speech, Part i. end of Scene 2.

the spirit of the piece informs the dramatization, which is as effective as it is fragmentary.
The scenes convey an impression of the stir of
throbbing humanity, and are instinct with life,
as if the kindling humanistic ideal, in its search
for expression, had scattered itself in vivid dramatic sparks.

The play remains unfinished, but its drift is
clear, and may be further inferred from the analogy
of *Sardanapalus.* The ardent ambition of Bourbon is closed in death, and this is probably significant of the general catastrophe. The material
triumph would have rested with Cæsar, the apparent loss with Arnold and Olimpia, yet not without
suggestion of some wider issue yet to be, pregnant
with redeeming possibilities of hope and the
after triumph of the good.

Sardanapalus, in its union of blending interests, is the most rounded and complete of all
Byron's dramas. Unlike the others, it moves in a
domain that is on earth but not of it—that
domain which is supremely represented in *Lear*

—in which things of sense are used as symbols
to suggest something beyond them, and the earthly
experience is made, by the exercise of a poet's
highest mood, to pass into the spiritual. And
the result is the more noteworthy as the external
theme is peculiarly congenial to Byron's imaginative genius, and the inner spiritual motive the
exposition of his highest and most chastened
mood. As a corollary, the dramatic development,
though faulty, gains in coherence, and the characters are drawn with Shakespearian fulness.

This is our poet's drama of Reconciliation, the
redemption, under Byronic conceptions, of a human
soul poised between the opposing impulses of good
and evil. To heighten the dramatic interest this
inner theme, with its deeper meaning, is blended
and contrasted with an external action of imposing significance, which connects it with the Fall
of Assyria, until both merge in the common catastrophe, the soul only attaining its final purification as the material splendour fades and perishes.

The whole struggle centres about Sardanapalus;

and since the contest is to be final, full sway must
be given to the opposing principles, and there must
be no compromise that could lead to a negation,
as with the baffled ideal of *Cain* or the bemocked
ideal of the *Deformed Transformed*.   Byron has
therefore finely represented the side of evil by an
implied impunity.   Sardanapalus is the personification of a soul rapt away from all temptations
save such as shall steep it in a spiritual Nirvana.
Within his reach, but luring him in vain, are the
power over a world-empire which he will not grasp,
the glory of conquest which stirs not his blood,
and the secrets of a mysterious religion of which
he disdains to inquire.   The murmurs of humanity, reaching him vaguely and from afar, move
him with no promptings of revolt, but only with
a half-querulous disquiet.   His very amiability is
a lassitude, his very pleasures a semi-conscious
dream.   Thus opens the first part of the drama.
The only problem as to this benumbed soul is
whether there exists in it some fibre which can
respond to any voice of hope and good.   Accord-

ingly these voices are represented by the poet with
peculiar force through two characters, who together
typify the nobler nature that only slumbers in
Sardanapalus.   Salemenes appeals to all that
answers in him to the sentiment of manhood or
duty; Myrrha to all the finer sensibilities of his
spirit.   On Myrrha therefore hinges the deeper
ethical interest of the drama.   The keynote of
her character is purity, and this runs like a silver
thread through the whole piece, condescending to
without being contaminated by the corruption of
Sardanapalus.   Thus Salemenes can only exhort
and die, but Myrrha continually ennobles and
purifies, until she makes one with her own, even
after death, the spirit she has enfranchised.

Assailed by these better voices, there needs
but the dramatically feeble conspiracy of Beleses
and Arbaces to wake Sardanapalus from his
lethargy.   Here begins the second step of the
drama, and here for a moment both the external
and internal actions meet in a quickened activity.
For it is the manhood in Sardanapalus that is at

first aroused, and deeds naturally attest the stirring of this new life. The combat brings out in him the traits of courage, nobility and magnanimity, the germs of which had been dramatically suggested in the former part ; and at his side, Salemenes and Myrrha grow to a momentary oneness in their devotion, which now manifests itself in deeds that leave no room for words.

But the redemption of Sardanapalus can be effected by no earthly expiation, and to death, with the opening of the third part, the action inevitably hastens. But as the external catastrophe rushes on, the inner struggle ceases, until, as the trumpet of Pania sounds, announcing the consummation of Assyria's doom, it becomes but the signal to apply the lamp to the pyre which shall light Myrrha and Sardanapalus "to the stars" (viii.).

The spiritual side of the drama must be clearly grasped, or its motive is stultified and its full import lost. Byron assuredly intended more than a material consummation ; and if his larger solution

(viii.) Act v. Scene i.

of the moral problem appears vague and dubious, this is only because it reflects the hesitancy of his own belief. The key-note of this solution is given in the words of Myrrha, when she says of their "commingling ashes:"

> "Pure as is my love to thee, shall they,
> Purged from the dross of earth, and earthly passion,
> Mix pale with thine." (ix.)

And the same idea of purification is suggested by the words of Sardanapalus himself, when he looks forward to rejoining his fathers

> "It may be, purified by death from some
> Of the gross stains of too material being;"—

or refers to the flame that will consume him as

> " . . that absorbing element
> Which most personifies the soul as leaving
> The *least of matter* unconsumed before
> Its fiery workings." (i.)

With the purification of Sardanapalus the spiritual struggle ends, for by it he has attained to the possession of his nobler nature; and since anything in the shape of reward would sully his victory he is content to rest simply on the thought

(ix.) Act v. Scene i.　　　　　(i.) *Ibid.*

of expiation (ii.).   But in a drama of so ethical
a scope, the possible extinction of a soul at the
moment it has regained its true nature would be
felt as intolerable, besides implying the very
material consummation which the poet wished to
avoid.   Hence the hint, the needful intimation
put into the mouth of the ever-helpful Myrrha.
For she has before said she will be ever at his
side—"Here and hereafter if the last may be,"—
and has assured him of their meeting again, if,
in her own words, "there be, *as I believe*, A
shore beyond the Styx" (iii.).   The hope, therefore,
of a continued activity for this nobler nature, the
"glory of going on and still to be," upheld by
that "pure love" to which it owed its recovery—
such is the higher issue to which this drama of
reconciliation dimly points.

(ii.) *Sard.*   "I am not
            Now to be pitied; or far more for what
            Is past than present;—for the future, 'tis
            In the hands of the deities, if such
            There be: I shall know soon; Farewell—Farewell."
                                          Act v. Scene i.

(iii.) Act iv. Scene i, and Act iii. Scene i.

The dramatization in this tragedy is from its
nature twofold. The characters group themselves
about the central idea—the regeneration of Sardanapalus; but in working out this end become
also dramatic in the stricter sense, and abound
in striking personal and individual traits. Sardanapalus himself, like Cain, is the exponent
of an idea, but, unlike Cain, is also set before
us with those more intimate touches that reveal
the individual man. He stands out "another
Antony," whether in revel (Act i. Scene 2) or
in fight ("The king, the king fights as he
revels ho!"); his Epicureanism is mingled in
the very spirit of nature with mitigating human
foibles, (iv.) his courage is allied to a lofty
nobility (v.) and magnanimity; (vi.) with all his
folly he is clearsighted, (vii.) with all his selfish-

(iv.) "I feel a thousand. . ."—Act i. Scene 2.

(v.) "Fate made me. . ."—*Ibid.* "Our annals. . ."—Act iv.
Scene 1.

(vi.) "Your swords and persons. . ."—Act ii. Scene 1. "He's
right. . ."—Act v. Scene 1.

(vii.) "Yes—stay a moment. . ."—Act ii. Scene 1.

ness can sorrow for a friend; (viii.) his mind is alive to humour (ix.) and quick to feel a passing flash of jealousy (i.). Myrrha, the soul of the piece in her love, devotion and patriotism, is also the woman who is deeply sensitive of her honour, (ii.) full of tender regrets, (iii.) and not without a touch of feminine vindictiveness (iv.), Salemenes is an inspiring influence, but he is also a heroic soldier, true to the death (v.). The lesser characters serve to intensify the action of the chief persons. Pania and his fellows rise to the inspiring example set by Salemenes, and emulate his valour; Zarina, the gentle, wronged queen, echoes with less force of character the devotion of Myrrha, and is also the wife who displays individual fortitude and good sense (vi.).

(viii.) "But fatal. Oh! my brother!"—Act v. Scene 1.

(ix.) "And the most tiresome. . ."—Act iii. Scene 1.

(i.) "Myrrha! what, at whispers. . ."—*Ibid.*

(ii.) "Thou hast no more eyes. . ."—Act i. Scene 2. "And I feel it. . ."—Act iv. Scene 1.

(iii.) "I weep not. . ."—Act i. Scene 2.

(iv.) "So sanguinary? Thou!. . ."—Act ii. Scene 1.

(v.) Act v. Scene 1.

(vi.) Act iv. Scene 1.

Arbaces and Beleses are weaker, but serve as foils—the one to Salemenes, the other to Sardanapalus. Arbaces is the blunt soldier who revolts from the king he supposed to be effeminate; (vii.) Beleses, as a person, is the converse of Sardanapalus in his superstition, weak ambition and ungenerous thirst of power (viii.).

Twofold also is the imaginative web into which this spiritual drama is woven, the material and moral aspects blending together as warp and woof. Assyria, vast, mysterious, remote and crashing slowly to its fall, is brought before us bathed in the light that never was on sea or land. This effect is chiefly produced and kept before the mind through the person of Beleses, who, as priest of "all Chaldæa's starry mysteries," is continually suggestive of the grandeur of the sun-deity and the awe of a mysterious religion. Myrrha lends a strand of a different kind. Her

---

(vii.) "Peace, factious priest, and faithless soldier ! . . ."—Act ii. Scene 1.

(viii.) *Ibid.*

inward purity has also an outward beauty corresponding to it.   She is not only the enfranchising
spirit but the *Greek* captive, the "eloquent Ionian,"
whose speech is music; and as such her words
and her presence breathe a vivifying charm,
which invests the barbarian grandeur and vast-
ness of Assyria with an added touch of ideal
Greek beauty.   Nature is also contributory to
these imaginative hues.   Sardanapalus' comparison
of the stars to Myrrha's eyes is an enhancement
of the idea suggested by her beauty (ix.).   Similarly,
in Beleses' speech (i.) on the setting sun ("'Tis
the furthest Hour of Assyria's years, and yet how
calm!"), the portentous stillness of the external
scene is made to reflect the spiritual Nirvana of
Sardanapalus, and accentuate the sense of coming
doom—a doom which Sardanapalus' dream, (ii.)
though wanting in true imaginative power, helps
to foreshadow.   And towards the end, Myrrha's
whole soliloquy (iii.) as she watches "The sunrise

(ix.) Act ii. Scene 1.   (i.) Act ii. opening of Scene 1.
(ii.) Act iv. Scene 1.   (iii.) Act v. opening of Scene 1.

which may be our last," impresses on us the
dreadful nearness and reality of that doom in
terms read from the glorious sky-pageant.

Closely connected with the imaginative conception, and as it were forming a part of it, is
the philosophic strain which runs through the
piece. The ideas of awe and mystery that centre
about the fall of Assyria and the fate of Sardanapalus are applied by an extended application
to the larger problem of being, and are reiterated,
like a continuous refrain, in reflections on the
" labyrinth of mystery called life "—the " fatal
penalties " imposed on it, (iv.) its littleness, (v.)
its slavery to circumstance, (vi.) its strange kinship
with sleep; (vii.) or on life's counterpart, death—
its naturalness, (viii.) its commonness, (ix.) its
powerlessness to hurt (i.).

(iv.) Act i. Scene 2.
(v.) " Must I consume my life. . ."—*Ibid.*
(vi.) " My gentle, wrong'd Zarina. . ."—Act iv. Scene 1.
(vii.) Opening speech.—*Ibid.*
(viii.) " To die is no less natural. . ."—Act i. Scene 2.
(ix.) " Save *one deed.* . ."—Act v. Scene 1.
(i.) " I know no evil. . ."—Act iv. Scene 1.

In the third group of dramas the developement of the idea is identical in theory with the developement of the characters; in other words, the dramatic action and the ideal action coincide. Accordingly the characters, as being themselves the architects of their destiny, tend to fill a larger space, the choric parts disappear, and the dramatic action enlarges. As regards the general conceptive treatment, nature is all but lost sight of in the growing human interest, and the thought and imagination blend in a philosophy that springs from the human action.

But in practice, Byron adjusts his characters explicitly to a motive too partial and narrow, and only implicitly to the inspiring idea that really fires his genius. Hence the strange and remarkable result of a dramatization that seems chaotic, and characters that beat the air vainly, moved by an aimless passion.

This result is however not surprising when looked at more closely. It is evident that a drama of

idea implies intensity of conception and a corresponding tension in the mind of the conceiver,
whereas a historical play demands variety and a
complete disengagement on the part of the dramatist. An idea set loose to play among politics
awakes all personal bitternesses, excites the spirit
of partizanship, and issues in rhetoric declamation
instead of true passion. There is, however, one
exception. When a mere political idea merges into
a national sentiment or aspiration it at once
becomes dramatic and capable of imaginative
treatment. The *Persians* and *William Tell* are
examples of dramas based on such a national
ideal; and they are successful because the
idea round which each centres has ceased to
represent what is merely individual and pro-
vincial, and becomes invested with a significance that gives it a permanent and universal
interest.

Byron, if the term was ever applicable to any
one, was the " patriot " of oppressed Europe—the
poet of all others who could have given dramatic

voice to the aspirations of the nations, or, in other words, applied the theory of Dipsychus, the struggle between the principles of freedom and oppression, to peoples as he had to individuals. This was the idea that burned within him, seeking only a fit subject. Unfortunately, from a lack of artistic perception proportioned to his poetic instincts, he declined upon motives inadequate and appealing only too easily to his purely personal sympathies, and, beyond this, hampered himself by a special adherence to the perversely false system of the unities. The result of this contradiction is the historical plays, which are none the less interesting as at once the most elaborate failure of their author and the most triumphant vindication of his genius. Apply to this surging and disordered passion the real motive or conception that gave it birth, and it yields up at once the secret of its meaning and its power.

The true guiding conception of *Marino Faliero* is not the vengeance that seeks satisfaction for a private injury, but the baffled revolt of a noble nature against political oppression (ii.). Taught by his own wrongs he learns those of the people —" What I suffer Has reached me through my pity for the people "—and falls in a desperate endeavour that aims at liberating them from the tyranny of a class and regaining for them civic freedom (iii.). The actual conspiracy, however, is dwarfed in the pourtrayal of the wrongs that lead to it, and hence invective rules throughout, as in the *Two Foscari*. But whereas in the latter

(ii.) The following lines would well represent the true motto of the play :

> " Yes, proud city !
> Thou must be cleansed of the black blood which makes thee
> A lazar-house of tyranny. . . .
> Let me but prosper and I make this city
> Free and immortal."—Act iii. Scene 1.

And cf. :

> " I will resign a crown, and make the state
> Renew its freedom—but oh ! by what means ?
> The noble end must justify them. What
> Are a few drops of human blood ? 'tis false,
> The blood of tyrants is not human."—Act iv. Scene 2.

And the whole speech beginning :

> "A spark creates the flame—'tis the last drop . . ."—
> Act v. Scene 1.

(iii.) Cf. the whole speech : " You see me here . . .;" and more especially the lines beginning : " Our private wrongs have sprung from public vices . . ."—Act iii. Scene 2.

drama the passion is individual and personal, in the former it is placed in the mouth of the Doge, the head and central figure of a great and populous state, the direct representative of the people, and is thus identified with the emotion and aspiration of a *nation*. This idea culminates in the final speech of the Doge : " I speak to Time and to Eternity, Of which I grow a portion, not to man," (iv.) a speech that is the last protest of one who " sought to free the groaning nations " (Act v. Scene 1), where the tone becomes comprehensive and prophetic, and the triumphant vengeance of oppressed and corrupted nationalities seems to throb and pulsate.

But this vain struggle of the patriot for freedom involves also disaster to the state he rules, ruin to the order of which he is a member, and destruction to the friends he loves; and hence he is deeply wounded in his patriotism, his early associations, his affections. What wonder then that with the keen cry of the invective there

(iv.) Act v. Scene 3.

mingles his utterance of Coriolanus-like contempt for "these slaves," these "stung plebeians"
whom he can scarcely stoop to lead; (v.) that he
has "wept and trembled at the thought of this
dread duty;" that pity almost overwhelms him
as he thinks of those who were his friends ere
they became his subjects, who revelled with him
or "sorrowed side by side," and whose lives, in
spite of "weak false remorse," engendered by
"feelings of old days," he is about to take by
stealth; (vi.) and that the anguish of his soul
breaks forth in the Othello-like outburst: "never
more—oh! never, never more," o'er "the blighted
old age of Faliero shall Sweet Quiet shed her
sunset!" (Act ii. Scene 1.)

Angiolina is the perfect wifely counterpart of
Faliero, and an almost completely dramatic character, inasmuch as being a woman she is drawn
only indirectly into the action, but displays her

(v.) Act iii. Scenes 1 & 2.

(vi.) Cf. especially the speech beginning: "Ye, though ye know
and feel our mutual mass," &c.—Act iii. Scene 2.

whole nature in relation to the protagonist. She is a kind of sterner, colder Desdemona to this Othello so injured in his country, whose assured dignity and innocence beyond suspicion respond to the pride and austerity of her husband. She has not, like Myrrha, to raise another from abasement or to regret it in herself, (vii.) but meets nobility with nobility from the first. We have but to imagine Faliero playing an adequate *rôle* as a patriot to see how surely her cold constancy would have seconded his " eternity of purpose." Like him, in the true patriot temper, she has "that within which shall o'ermaster all; " and at the last, when her brief appeal for pity fails to move his judges, she can uphold his resolution in what should be his martyrdom, with the words :

" Then die, Faliero ! since it must be so."—Act v. Scene 1.

In proportion as the character of Marino is referred to the real actuating motive, it gains in

(vii.) Cf. " Suspect *me !* " &c.—Act ii. Scene I.

power and consistency, and draws the minor characters as well within the bounds of stricter
dramatic relation. But this leads to yet a fresh
revelation. As the characters approach to the distinctness that comes of being swayed by a vivifying ideal, they tend *ipso facto* to become living
and individual creations, making it impossible
to doubt that could Byron have struck upon a
fortunate and comprehensive idea he might have
produced a historical drama of great and varied
and truly dramatic interest. This was partially
the case in the semi-historical *Sardanapalus*; it
is still more so with *Marino*. Apart from other
conditions, the character of the Doge as a man is
drawn with extraordinary power. His fiery outbursts and compunctions as a patriot prepare us
for his poignant laments as a citizen and a
son, (viii.) and lead up to the more intimate traits
of his character—his persistency of resolve, (ix.)

(viii.)   Cf. Act iii. Scene i. Opening speech.

(ix.)   " All things wear in him
        An aspect of eternity," &c.—Act ii. Scene I.

his noble qualities and generous failings, (i.) his calmness in action, (ii.) his gentleness, (iii.) his quick and active sympathy (iv.). Still more striking is the unexpected sobriety and impersonality of the treatment. This appears in the scene (v.) —in itself so dramatic—between the Doge and Angiolina, in which the traits of both are vividly brought out, and may be specially illustrated by the Doge's encomium on virtue (vi.). And consistent with this clear character-painting is the Shakespearian tone that rings throughout this play, as if the bold conception had wrung from the poet, in his own despite, the appropriate larger dramatic utterance. To the speech on virtue and those outbursts recalling an Othello or a Coriolanus already quoted, a few other passages may be added. In one, we seem to hear a

(i.) "I love all noble qualities," &c.—Act ii. Scene 1.
(ii.) "It was ever thus," &c.—Act iv. Scene 2.
(iii.)   " Come then,
     My gentle child," &c.—Act ii. Scene 1.
(iv.) "How fares it with you?" &c.—*Ibid.*
(v.) Act ii. Scene 1.
(vi.) "Where is honour," &c.—*Ibid.*

Portia pleading, or the very voice of Isabella as she makes her vain appeal to Angelo; (vii.) in another Othello again speaks; (viii.) while the Doge's apostrophe to the ducal cap (ix.) recalls instantly the very spirit of that of Prince Henry to the royal crown.

What has been said generally of *Marino Faliero* applies with even greater force to *The Two Foscari*, for the broader human issues of the former are attenuated in the latter to mere individual interests too weak to sustain the historical structure imposed on them.

The virtual idea on which *The Two Foscari* rests is again the assertion of human freedom

(vii.)   " Alas ! signor,
He who is only just is cruel ; who
Upon the earth would live were all judged justly ? "
                              —Act v. Scene I.
(viii.) " Farewell all social memory," &c.—Act iii. Scene 2.
(ix.)   " Hollow bauble !
Beset with all the thorns that line a crown,
Without investing the insulted brow
With the all-swaying majesty of kings,
Thou idle, gilded, and degraded toy,
Let me resume thee as I would a vizor."
                              Act i. Scene 2.

against political oppression—but oppression conceived, not as affecting the state, but as ruining,
frustrating and desolating the life of the individual citizen. And since this idea responds
to an only too congenial chord in the mind of
the dramatist, there is mingled with the hopeless
conception of political misery a bitter, fatalistic
view of life which finds expression in an iterated
strain of personal anguish.

The idea, so far as it is capable of developement, is vividly presented in the person of the
protagonist Foscari, and accentuated in the characters of the Doge and Marina. The Doge is
as it were a background of mute, feeble, pathetic
suffering—an incarnate hopelessness, a dumb protest against human wrongs. To him it seems
"we must have sinned in some old world, and
this is hell;" and the earth, he says, "though
loaded with marble," will lie far lightlier on his
heart than "the thoughts which press it now."
Foscari himself, regarded strictly in the light of
the idea, is an intense and lyrical voice of

anguish crying inarticulately against the state
injustice and tyranny that crush him as a citizen
and the harsh destiny that overwhelms him as a
man. "Nothing can sympathize with a Foscari"
is the key-note of his passion; and his unmeasured transports are such as rise naturally to
the lips of a man who cannot charge his memory
"with much save sorrow," and who has been so
visited that he must "needs think" that he
"was wicked." There is, however, that in his
fate which lends it a general interest, for, in his
own words: "My doom is common; many are
in dungeons" (Act iii. Scene i.). Marina is the
most completely dramatic character, because, like
Angiolina, her action relates less to the tragedy
than to its consequences in another. Thus the
anguish which Foscari vents is echoed back by
Marina with the shriller sensitiveness that betokens the woman, and the fiercer personal indignation of the wife who feels herself injured
in her husband. "I have proved the worst,"
she exclaims, "in the infernal process of my

poor husband." Her love for him, "exiled,
mangled, persecuted" as he is, is absolute. For
him she would willingly have given her blood;
and could courage have saved him, there is that
in her heart which "would make its way through
hosts with levelled spears." Her defiance of
Loredano is couched in the same lioness-like
strain; and when she thinks of the enemies to
whom her lord's sufferings are due—sufferings so
great that even Foscari "cannot wish them *all*
they have inflicted"—the smothered passion of her
hate flashes out in the indignant rejoinder:

> "*All!* the consummate fiends! a thousandfold,
> May the worm which ne'er dieth feed upon them!"—
> Act iv. Scene i.

This play is a notable example of the extent
to which Byron's dramatic strength depends on
the guidance of a conceptive idea. As an historical drama the play remains inarticulate. For
Foscari's so-called love of country is, in Marina's
words, "passion and not patriotism;" and even
this weak motive is further weakened and con-

fused by the sub-plot of the vengeance of Loredano, on which so much turns. Yet once allow
that Foscari's passion has a sufficient motive, and
how dramatic does it become; and when it is
really not aimless, but can ally itself with the
passing situation, as in Marina's defiance of
Loredano (i.), how powerful is the effect produced! But in one instance the passion coincides
for a moment with the main action itself, and
the result is a sustained scene of the keenest
pathos (ii.).

Conversely it may be noticed how the characters, once conceived in reference to an adequate
motive, tend to develop living, individual traits.
Both Foscari and Marina live, dramatically, too
absorbed in their suffering to exhibit any other
qualities than the mutual devotion that springs
from it; but the sorrow of the old Doge, subdued as it is, allows more scope for the painting
of character, and his individuality is brought

(i.) Act iii. Scene 1.
(ii.) Foscari's death. — Act iv. Scene 1.

before us by a few slight but subtle touches—such, for instance, as his pathetic avowal that he begins "to fail in apprehension and Wax very old—old almost as my years" (Act v. Scene i.), and his dying exclamation: "A sovereign should die standing" (*Ibid.*). Loredano, again, considered apart from the general action, and in reference to the special motive that actuates him, is a consistent and clearly drawn character. His life, too, resolves itself into a single passion—that of vengeance; and the violence with which this purpose possesses him, and the sleuth-hound tenacity with which he works it out, are summed up with suggestive power in the concluding lines of the play:

" *Chief of the Ten.*   What debt did he owe you?
Loredano.   A long and just one; Nature's debt and *mine.*"

Two "Nature" passages (iii.) in the historical plays have a significance which might easily be overlooked.   They have been called undramatic,

---

(iii.) Lioni's speech in *Marino Faliero* (Act iv. Scene i), and Foscari's speech in *The Two Foscari* (Act i. Scene i).

yet are hardly so. In the stress of human emotion the poet turns as it were for relief to nature, and by the implied contrast enhances our sense of the world's strife. But whereas, in Lioni's speech, the contrast lies between the calm and silence of night and the restless existence of men, and thus accords with the motive of the piece, to Foscari, the suffering and persecuted *man*, the beauty of the scene just as appropriately suggests only an added bitterness of personal loss in the reminiscences it calls up of his lost boyhood.

Werner may fairly be called the dregs of the Byronic drama. It displays Byron at his worst, shorn of the conditions that constitute his strength, but by this weakness reveals the sources of that strength and explains the method of its activity. Without the impulse of some stimulating idea Byron's genius fails to give life to its creations, and, to supply the defect, falls back on facile imitation, and yields to its besetting temptation of substituting vulgar mystery for imaginative effect, and complication of incident for true dramatic developement. These tendencies were visible in *Manfred* and to some extent in the *Deformed Transformed*, in both of which imitation of Goethe was apparent. But in *Manfred* the crude husk veiled a kernel of beauty, and in the *Deformed Transformed* genius broke lightly through its self-imposed trammels. In *Werner* the husk remains without the beauty, and the genius is strangled in the trammels. It is a kind of sixth-rate *Robbers*, and breathes the spirit of all that is most trivial in German robber-romance.   Byron's initial mistake lay in taking what was an excellent *moral tale*, (iv.) and endeavouring to re-cast it, untransfigured by imagination, as a drama.   The subject thus treated lends itself only too readily to the

(iv.). This was the *German's Tale*, written by a Miss Lee. As showing the tendency of one side of Byron's genius, the following words, taken from the poet's *Preface* to this drama, are by no means without significance: "When I was young (about fourteen, I think), I first read this tale, which made a deep impression upon me; and may indeed be said to contain the germ of much that I have since written."

commonplace of Byron's philosophy, and, borne up
by no living ideal, remains low and on the ground.

The idea of *Werner* is that of *Manfred* diluted
—the succumbing to the worse of a weak soul to.
whom it was easily open to have chosen the
better. Werner, or Siegendorf, is but a kind of
attenuated Manfred. "Yellow sickness sits ca-
verned in his eye," but it speaks only of a wasted
life and is the mark of no inward strivings of
thought. Perplexed by no Hamlet-like doubts
he gives vent to no Hamlet-like musings, but,
feebly inveighing against the harshness and
tyranny of a world he has made for himself,
drifts querulously to his doom.

The nothingness of this sick existence finds
an echo in those general reflections on feudal
tyranny and the sufferings of the poor which
are scattered through the play, (v.) and is
more specially accentuated in the characters of
Gabor and Idenstein. The former is vaguely

(v.)   Cf. Josephine's speech, " I fain," &c. (Act i. Scene I, near
end) ; and Gabor's speech, " There goes," &c. (Act ii. end of Scene I).

drawn, but the key-note of his personality seems
to be given in the words: "Oh, thou world!
Thou art indeed a melancholy jest!" and this
strain is only continued on a more mocking note
by Idenstein, whose humour—not without a certain genial breadth—is but the Byronic comment
in its most flippant mood. Josephine, as the
sympathetic wife, is the most dramatic character,
but her personality is conditioned by that of
Werner, and her feeble complaints against the
world are the echo of his. Ida is too slight to
have much significance. A dramatization that
is truly a moralization, and hardly needing the
words of Werner to point the moral: "Take heed
. . . you have seen to what the passions led
me." (Act iv. Scene 1).

The ideal theme proving insufficient, the action
falls back on plot and mystery. This side of
Manfred is represented, still in diluted form,
through Werner's son Ulric, whose likeness to
his prototype is completed by his being "a
forester and breather Of the steep mountain-

tops" (Act iv. Scene 1). Ulric is really what some critics have supposed all Byron's dramatic characters to be—the personification of the Giaour —Conrad—Lara sentiment; and for us, in his combination of the most objectionable Byronic traits, is an admirable type of all that the best of Byron's characters are *not*.

This exhibition of Byron at his lowest is not without its reward for criticism. Shorn of his characteristic excellences, he shows the solid foundations of his strength. In this weakest of dramas there is yet an inherent elemental force that expands not rarely into dramatic life, as for instance in Werner's awakening remorse, (vi.) or Idenstein's exaltation at the possession of the jewel (vii.), or Stralenheim's presentiments (viii.). The play is throughout unreal and fantastic, yet it gives the impression of having been created not artificially, but by a natural and spontaneous effort of the mind.

(vi.). "And now your remedy!" &c.—Act iii. Scene 1.
(vii.). "Oh, thou sweet sparkler!" &c.—*Ibid.*
(viii.). Act iii. Scene 2.

V.

SUCH, in essential outline, is the analysis of a group of dramatic poems which stand out in all literature as unique and astonishing—unique, because as no others do, they achieve success by means which seem incompatible with success; astonishing, because while they distinctly produce a certain effect of disenchantment, they yet lay a constraining spell even upon spirits most antithetic to the poet's own. No portraiture can make of Byron one of those imposing and majestic figures the particular defects of which are lost in the larger symmetry of the whole; yet in reading him we reach glimpses of what is imposing and majestic, and have the consciousness that these qualities are the faithful reflection of an inherent element in the poet's mind. And it is this indefinable element of power which preserves to dramas devoid of that deliberate perfection which could make of them artistic wholes a place among those greatest poems which are "possessions for all time," and asserts for them their meed of recognition when such are spoken of.

This element, which it is plain must constitute the very basis, the essential character of the poet's genius, has hitherto been only generally alluded to or indirectly indicated as implicitly contained in his method. For a poet's method can never remain a bare and isolated fact. It is simply his individuality, that whereby he is original—is himself and not another; but at the same time it is a manifestation, an indication of some reserve-power of which that individuality is but the shaping expression. So much, in a vague and general way, might be inferred from the foregoing analysis, which revealed a mind instinctively attracted to certain leading ideas, yet displaying in their developement rich and varied qualities which seemed to flow from some latent and unexplained source. If, then, this latent power could be defined with sufficient clearness and should prove to be such that all the manifestations can be deduced from it, while it accords with and explains them, we should have arrived at an estimate of Byron's genius that might claim to be consistent and complete, and at the same time serve as a criterion for bringing to a decisive test the leading charges that affect his greatness as a poet generally.

The basis of Byron's genius, the distinguishing character that ranks it with that of the few sovereign poets, is its universality—that which, speaking in a broad sense, might almost be identified with that spirit in the poet which is correlative with humanity.   He is the universal poet whose sympathy with human feeling is most searching, most far-reaching and profound.   But if we wish to use the term in a more determinate sense, as connoting certain cardinal poetic qualities, we must define it as the faculty that *tends* to realize most largely poetic truth.   As such it is both conceptive and executive.   As a conceptive mood its tendency is to view things not as isolated, but in their relations; as an instrument, to express adequately what it conceives. Moreover this conception is necessarily conditioned by seriousness or morality, and implies thought working sanely on a cosmos subject to the laws of thought, and imagination which, while suggesting and combining, is based on truth, rising always from the known to the unknown.

This faculty may be further traced in its operation and results. Flowing from the poet as a poetic force, it creates by natural and spontaneous development, not by artifice and ingenuity; it allies itself mainly with what is great and persistent and truly human, as opposed to what is trivial, fleeting and capricious; and it is ever concerned with the inward meanings of things, not their mere outward shows and effects.

A tendency in the poet, a potentiality in his work, this universal quality, announced by a few great definite characters, must itself ever remain indeterminate. It may be even very imperfect, yet, being imperfect, is always tending to perfection. Hence, in those poets it informs, the

prevailing impression of a general power apart
from particular beauties or particular defects; of
a leaven modifying the work without destroying
the individuality. Thus it has among others
Shakespeare for its Proteus, Marlowe for its Giant
audaciously heaping Pelion on Ossa, Keats for its
Marcellus untimely snatched; and Goethe we
have called its Olympian, and Byron its fitful
and fevered Prometheus. And in none of the
great, diverse band of whom these are types is
its presence felt to be more remarkable than in
Byron, as in no one was the personality so pronounced, the faults so great, the perturbing
influences so powerful; but in none the potential
force so clearly to be traced, manifesting itself
unequally, irregularly, but ever surely from the
rudest beginning up to a stage where death
quenches it, still immature and still maturing.
The *Tales* are Byron's genius in its simplest
expression. Had he written nothing besides these
he must 'still have been remembered as the pos-
sessor of a passionate and on-sweeping force

unparalleled in literature, but a force ending in itself and embalming no human interest. In *Juan* and its kindred group this force becomes living, and girdling the whole of human life in a chain of mocking laughter and tears, reveals Byron as the greatest satirist to whom imagination ever lent its flashing terror. But satire belittles, and with all its power misses the true note of greatness. This missing note is fully struck in *Harold*, in the finest cantos of which Byron's force allies itself with all that is great and pathetic in the world of man and the world of nature. Gradually nature recedes from his view, leaving the vision of humanity alone in all the interactions of its struggle with destiny. Then a fresh light kindles within him ; his force developes yet anew, and by a final transmutation passes into the expression of dramatic emotion. (i.).

In his possession of this inspired force, growing out of the union of a full poetic vision and the power of rendering it, Byron touches and is

(i.) Cf. Note at end.

akin to Shakespeare—is one with him in the
kind of his genius, however inferior in degree.
That he was far inferior in degree is to be at
once admitted; and the nature of his inferiority
may be inferred from that side of his genius
which gave it its individual traits. The grand
method of Shakespeare was—to have none. With
him, the faculty of representation so exactly poises
the faculty of vision that his creations seem like
those of nature—are such, that is, that they
can scarcely be conceived as being other than
they are. At what point of contact Shakespeare's
sympathy first touches his subject we may conjecture but cannot know. He is veiled, though
somewhere in his works Shakespeare *is*, if the
requisite knowledge to find him were ours.
Byron is unveiled, and having the requisite
knowledge, we can trace him in his work, and
know that the point at which he approached his
subject was *personal sympathy.* Some emotion
he has himself felt, some experience he has himself realized seems necessary to kindle his genius

into action, but once kindled, it works as freely, as spontaneously, as naturally as that of Shakepeare himself. It not only penetrates but glows and irradiates. The personality of Byron stirs the deeps of thought as a stone that is thrown into the water spreads a circle about it. Led at first, like Shakespeare, like Goethe, to interpret what he sees through the bias of his own spirit, the interpretation grows and widens with what it works on, until, though ever swayed by that spirit, it becomes a part of a spirit mightier still, and renders back, for all such limitation, the voice of humanity itself, which he has heard, the impression of the universe or cosmos, the vision of which has been revealed to him.

This is Byron's open secret, the explanation of the element of self or personality in him. It marks a limitation of his genius, but a limitation of degree only, not of kind. Byron is not only a lesser Shakespeare ; he is a lesser Shakespeare with aberrations. That which in Shakespeare is the nature and the very being is in

Byron the genius at its best and the tendency. Shakespeare is sometimes peccant; Byron is very often peccant. But with all his aberrations, his tendency is to the large and impartial method of nature; and though his power be inferior, it works, when at its best, like the power of Shakespeare.

This assignment of the personality of Byron to its due place in his work is the more important because it has been such a stumbling-block to criticism. Personality, as that which gives a poet's work its individual stamp or originality, is also that whereby he is most open to the shafts of criticism. The superficial foibles of a poet find their natural reflection in his verse, as those of ordinary men in their daily life; and his personality, as it matures, will always be the medium by which his genius approaches its subject. Still the personality is distinct from the genius; and not only this, but the genius may react upon it, modifying and ennobling it. This struggle is the history of every poet, but time and circumstance may introduce new factors to complicate it. Shake-

speare, living in an age of stormy energy but
robust faith, can subdue his personal emotion
to equanimity; Æschylus, poet of an empire-city
and prophet of a religion as yet firm-based, can
utter his thunders with an assured tone; Goethe,
a sage retired, looking before and after, will not
allow the present to seduce him from contemplation to action; but Byron, feeling in himself
and convulsed to the very centre by the storm
around him, cannot think without his thinking
passing into egoism. But this egoism does not
exclude his dramatic insight, it only conditions it.
His vision may be perturbed, never obscured. Had
Shakespeare—the Shakespeare of the sonnets, the
poet who, according to Voltaire, was an intoxicated
barbarian, according to M. Taine a man of superhuman passions—had this Shakespeare allowed
free play to all his thronging impulses ere he had
wholly subdued them to his saner judgment, a
rich and strange confusion would have shown the
result in his work; his world would have been
volcanic, but still dramatic. With Byron the con-

fusion is there, but it is the symbol of an inner force akin to Shakespeare's (ii.).

Nor must it be forgotten that Byron's weakness contains a compensating element of strength. The qualities that run down to defects run up to merits. His intensity adds to his dramatic expression in vividness what it takes from it in breadth; and his insistence on the idea withdraws meaning from the actors only to impress it more strongly on destiny. Where Shakespeare, therefore, represents impartially, leaving us to infer what we will, Byron calls up for us, as even Shakespeare has not done, presenting them as an artist, not a moralist, the great ideas, the great problems dear to the heart of humanity. And while in actual dramatic play he is inferior to Shakespeare, he is superior in this respect to Goethe, who in turn surpasses him in subtle representation of ideas. For Goethe, contemplating all by wisdom, and having at command the brightest spirit of poetry, is so absorbed in the delight of the

(ii.) Cf. Note at end.

problem that he condenses to a point long revolved
processes of thought, leaving action unregarded.

Turning from the poet to trace the operation
of this universal spirit in his work, we find it
modifying all that is merely individual in his
method, and betraying its presence by a thousand
subtle touches throughout the sphere of his
thought. Take his dramas as a group, and apart
from other imperfections, they appear so small in
content as to offer no basis for any superstructure
of theory. Take them as the partial manifestations of a universal and inexhaustible genius, and
they dilate into revelations surcharged with meaning. In the case of the foremost poets, the world
has had to distinguish between their quality and
their achievement; between the work they have
actually performed and the reserve-power which
that work implies. For us moderns, the fame of
Æschylus depends mainly on a trilogy and tra-
dition; without *Faust*, Goethe would find it hard
to make good his place; in Shakespeare alone the
world has been content to acknowledge a perfect

balance of power and achievement. But this only means that his achievement is more satisfying than that of other men, not that it is final. What is the meaning of the Shakespearian group of plays? It is a vast potentiality. The combinations formed by them imply the promise of other combinations as countless as the worlds of nature. And it is the same with the characters. Shakespeare's characters are not comprised by his actual creations. Lear, Macbeth, and the whole series of his persons suggest other series in endless progression, which we can almost imagine as existing in a spiritual world.

This is that same potentiality that reveals itself in the Byronic group of dramas too. They are not the last results of a vein of thought that has been worked out and exhausted, but vistas opened up into the mysterious depths of life in every direction whither the hoping, fearing, questioning human spirit can penetrate. In reading them, we are insensibly led from the particular subject into this universal life that sur-

rounds it.   Each drama burgeons with thoughts
that suggest thoughts beyond them, so that we
could easily conceive the group doubled or trebled,
and from the characters and scenes presented body
forth others as numerous.   In two most interesting cases it was possible actually to do this, and
without speculating on the details to conjecture
the manner in which Byron would have treated
the proposed subjects of *Francesca* and *Tiberius*.
A third instance is suggestive of still more important inferences, for although we can make no
guess as to the "way he had in view" for com-
posing the second part of *Heaven and Earth*,
we know that it must have demanded in the
highest degree the exercise of invention and
imagination.

Potentiality can also be inferred from the manner in which the dramas were produced.   The
speed with which they were written tells as much
for as against them.   They were not the elaborated
caprices of a passing mood, but the swift results
of lifelong   meditation—the   luxuriant   plants

springing lustily from a rich soil. This is confirmed by Byron's own words. He has told us
that *Prometheus*, his favourite type, dominated his
mind from boyhood, and that the subject of
Werner occupied his thoughts during many years.

The potentiality that informs the dramas as a
whole can be traced in detail; potentiality in
choice and treatment, in the structural development, in the characterization—potentiality in all
those elements into which the master-faculties of
thought and imagination enter. To touch Byron at
these points is to meet with a dramatist who is at
the beginning, not the end of his power, and whose
genius, through all passing deflections, works in
the natural, creative manner of Shakespeare.

Each of Shakespeare's dramas is a piece of
nature; each of Byron's the evolution of an
idea. Both these results are really identical,
although the means by which they are arrived
at differ. Byron's mastery begins with his choice
of a subject. He is as nobly rapacious as
Shakespeare himself. He never, like Hugo,

sets out from an arbitrary ethical motive, to
be worked out artificially to the smallest detail,
but seizes on some idea that floats to him
from the mysterious sea of humanity, and
makes all its germ-like issues expand. On this
expansion the dramatic interest wholly depends;
never on the details of a story or the intricacy
of a plot. This but describes Shakespeare's
method.   It is true, weaknesses beset Byron. He
would fain bend the idea to the yoke of the
unities; the subject conniving, he is tempted, and
indulges the spirit of revolt; some point allures
him, and he falls into pitfalls of "self."   But all
this is in vain against the native force of Byron's
genius, which carries him out of himself on the
tide of the rushing idea, with contributory mo-
mentum from the very faults—the personal motive
lending a passionate vitality, the revolt spirit a
fiery impulse—on to a close that is felt to be
natural, inevitable.   So that, for all defects, we
hesitate to lay hands on any part, lest in so doing
we should seem to be cutting a portion from a

living organism. Moreover, the close, which forms so important a part in most of the dramas, up-gathering into one final impression the whole meaning of the piece, always brings us full-tide with humanity, leaving the poet himself out of sight. The close of *Heaven and Earth* presents an unparalleled dramatic impression of the ruin of a universe, that of *Cain* of the doom of a whole race.   And even single figures such as Manfred or Sardanapalus, are never individuals merely, but types. Byron's genius is attested as much by his failures as his success.   In his inferior plays (which, broadly speaking, are his historical ones), the failure lies in the partial triumph of the false principle and the personal motive over the unconscious ideal of his genius. In these plays the potential power manifested is the same, but it is a power that surges blindly, having missed its aim.

The same with the scenery and incidents. Nothing is more astonishing in Byron than the ever-changing variety of external effect, except the

triumphant subjection of this to the inner meaning.
Byron passes from earth to heaven, from the real
to the imaginary, with the same imperial facility
as Shakespeare and the same imaginative mastery.
The tumult of *Lear*, the movement of *Macbeth*,
the incidents of *Hamlet* are but the external perturbations answering to the deeper hidden springs
of passion.   Just so the desolation of *Heaven and
Earth* is symbolic of the greater human agony;
the stir and clash of the *Deformed Transformed*
figurative of the noble strivings of the spirit; the
frenzied action of *Manfred* reflective of incurable
perturbations of soul.   Nor does it for an instant
move our wonder that we are borne now to the
spaces of the stars with Lucifer, now to the dream-
realm of Sardanapalus, now to the old-world palaces
of Venice.   There is nothing in all this to surprise,
because the power of the poet makes it seem
natural, inevitable.   The dramatic environment and
movement are to the idea as the body and its
movement to the soul; and where the former are
faulty we perceive that it is from want of vitality

in the latter; as for instance the coarsely con-. ceived *Hall of Arimanes* is a fit stage for those theatric spirits miscopied from Goethe; and the feeble action of *Werner* a consequence of the vulgar motive it embodies.

From the natural developement follows the homogeneity that nature alone can bestow. Each of the dramas has a glow, a living force, an inbreathed vitality, which no mere literary skill can give. Each is vested with an appropriate air of thought, each has a unity of sentiment. "Read," says Coleridge, "*Romeo and Juliet*, all is youth and spring." But read also the *Deformed Transformed*, all is nobility and grandeur; read *Cain*, all is intellectual splendour; read *Sardanapalus*, all is "light such as never was on sea or land." Each of Byron's dramas is a piece of nature.

But, it may be said, in the particulars of dramatization, in all that concerns the characters and their action and interaction, Byron is surely far inferior to Shakespeare. He is assuredly inferior. The quality of his dramatization is thinner, less

full, less copious than that of Shakespeare; but to
Shakespeare's it assimilates and asserts still its
sovereign potentiality.

No great dramatist, on pain of losing his claim
to that title, works "without a purpose and an
aim," conscious or unconscious. When, therefore,
Byron's dramatization is compared with that of
Shakespeare, it must be with constant reference
to the particular method on which it depends. It
must not be asked of Byron that he should perform what he never attempted to perform. All
drama presupposes characters and an end to which
they tend. And the ends which all great drama
proposes to itself are practically two—the ethical
end and the dramatic end, each of which may at
times practically coalesce with the other, or at
times assert an overshadowing predominance. The
question asked by the former is: "What is the
divine or natural law by which the currents of all
human action are governed?" The question asked
by the latter is: "Given actors, with certain
passions, what is the inevitable result to which

their actions tend?" The treatment of these questions depends on that quality in the poet which has been called seriousness or morality—that quality on which all his dramatic intuition hinges. Without it he may be a great writer or a great technical artist or any other meanly-great creature, but a great poet never. And in so far as, in his human fallibility, he falls short in it, in so far does he fall short of possible achievement. That a poet therefore should possess this quality is all-important. With reference to conventional morality he must be at least non-moral if not actually immoral; but a failure in that larger, higher moralty is fatal to him, for in proportion as it fails is the significance of the cosmos dimmer to his perception. Now Byron's method, the mode in which his genius seeks instinctive expression, presupposes chiefly an ethical end, but admits also a dramatic end; and the seriousness of his treatment of both is equally unexpected and striking. Man is Dipsychus. Tendencies of good and evil within him meet fatalistic tendencies of good and evil

without him. That, to Byron's mind, is the con-
stitution of things. Destiny governs all. But is
this destiny beneficent or otherwise? Is it a mere
Moloch, a monstrousness making for nothing, or
is there within it or beyond it that ordering Righte-
ousness which is present triumphantly with
Æschylus, serenely with Sophocles and Goethe,
and by implication with Shakespeare? The answer
to this only seems doubtful because Byron's aspiration is always clogged with doubt. Destiny
delights in showing him its implacable side, which
is thus most dramatically made the over-mastering
motive, so that the bitter ever seems to overpower
the sweet, despair to triumph over hope; life is a
struggle, and its watchword is not victory but
defeat. Yet after all the turbulence is only on
the surface. We might apply to Byron—the Byron
of *Juan* but also of *Cain*, the poet whose baser
instincts clashed vainly against his ideals—those
words of Festus to Paracelsus:

> " These low thoughts are no inmates of your mind,
> Or wherefore this disorder ? " (iii.)

(iii.) Browning's Paracelsus, Part iv.

Revolt is but the measure of the aspiration deep down in Byron's heart.   It is aspiration that speaks, in every cadence of sadness, through the mocking voices that interpret the worser side of Dipsychus; it is this that breathes in the spirit of such dramas as *Cain* and *Heaven and Earth,* which imply not revolt against eternal justice, but arraignment of the cruelty and injustice in the decrees imputed to it; and in *Sardanapalus,* his one noble drama of reconciliation, it is this that sounds darkly the possibilities of human redemption, and faintly intimates his trust in the larger hope.

The dramatic end is with Byron secondary to the ethical end, as the actor is secondary to the controlling destiny.   But it is only less important relatively.   For though Destiny shape the end, it is only through the passions of the actors that she does so.   Accordingly Byron fully recognizes passion as a dramatic motive in itself, and gives to it the same sway as does Shakespeare.   Happily this is not the place for a special vindication of Byron's life and character,—though one is fain to say, after

Goethe, that the energy even of ill-regulated passion may be preferable to that hyper-morality which
is as a dropsy destroying the life itself;—but it is
justifiable to note how in this particular the artist
throws light on the man.   Byron's sanity and
temperance in dealing with passion are as conspicuous as was his seriousness in regard to larger
ethical issues.   Though critics will not have it so,
Byron was not always in extremes.   Behind the
wayward and transported man stood the universal
artist, who "saw life steadily and saw it whole."
His life may be perturbed, but his conscience remains clear and undeceived.   If for nothing else
than this, it was worth while to turn for a moment
from the careless richness of his other work to the
neglected dramas, in which alone this nobler artistic
seriousness could find sway (iv.).

(iv.) I cannot refrain from calling attention here to what seems to
me the most striking instance in Byron of dramatic insight allying
itself with the ethical instinct in a single intuition.   In the last
words of the Doge (*Marino Faliero*, Act v. Scene 3) we have the very
utterance of a Hebrew prophet painting on an immediate dream-
future the absolute inevitable consequence of things conceived as
present in his consciousness.

In the first place, when dealing with guilt and error, Byron is impartial; he never palliates or excuses—never tries to make untruth seem truth. Manfred sins greatly, and his fall is as great. Cain is much tried, but he errs, and, erring, draws down immitigable ruin on others as well as himself. Given such characters, Shakespeare himself could not conduct them more inexorably to their inevitable end. And Byron's feeling is shown still more strongly in a case where he fails —in *Werner*. So clearly does the sense of Nemesis abide with him, that, as we have seen, for the moment he forgets the poet and the artist in the moralist, and with almost childlike *naïveté* bids us, through the mouth of the erring father: " Take heed . . . you have seen to what the passions led me." Secondly, he never dallies with passion or stoops to linger—for their own sake—on its baser or ignobler phases. This was remarkably shown in his foreshadowed conception of the character of Tiberius, and receives still fuller illustration by his emphatic rejection of love as a dramatic motive. Love in its most impassioned aspects he does portray; but, as we shall see when considering his heroines, it is not only made subordinate as a motive, but actually disappears in the wider issues of destiny.

Ordered by this profound seriousness and differentiated only by its adaptation to his method, Byron's dramatization proceeds uniformly and on the same natural lines of development as that of Shakespeare. The dramatic glances of Shakespeare and Byron, playing, as it were, from opposite points, meet and intersect. Shakespeare begins simply from the characters and developes them ethically and dramatically up to the catastrophe. Byron is entranced, first and foremost, with destiny, and traces her vacillating purpose down into the actions of the vacillating Dipsychus—man, who only after he has played the puppet to those eddyings of fate has time to exhibit dramatic individual traits. Characters, therefore, like Shakespeare's Byron has not and could not have drawn, but, as was said in speaking of his method,

character-groups dramatically interpretative of
some aspect of destiny he has drawn with a free
and sure hand. *Cain* may be taken as an instance of this. Cain himself, as compared with
Lucifer, is, necessarily, not sharply discriminated;
but Cain, together with Lucifer and the accessory
actors, completely carries out the idea of the
drama.

The persons being such lead to corresponding
dramatic effects in both dramatists. Shakespeare's
persons, by an infinite variety of combinations,
display themselves to us as tragic and comic
characters, whose interaction leads to definite
situations of pathos or humour. Byron's destiny-
groups, on the other hand, rather interpret for us
tragic or comic emotion itself, attractive of its
own appropriate scenic effect,—not, be it noted,
emotion in the abstract or coldly personified, but
the very pulsing passion or humour itself. This
follows necessarily from the Dipsychus conception,
which, narrow as it may seem beside the character
conception of Shakespeare, is yet pregnant with

all the infinite dramatic possibilities that flow
from contrast; for, as representative of what is
higher in man's soul, it draws within its range all
elements of pity and terror; as representative of
man's lower nature, all elements of the contrasting
ironic humour.   Compare the yearnings of Cain,
the aspirations of Arnold, the despair of Foscari,
the doubt of Sardanapalus.   Here are all the
germs of tragedy.   And, again, compare the lofty
scorn of Lucifer, the worldly sarcasm of Cæsar,
the levity of Sardanapalus in his lighter moments,
the coarser humour of Idenstein.   Here are all
the germs of comedy leading up to and blending
with tragedy.   From the dramatic action and interaction as thus conceived flow naturally the
scenes and situations.   These, as warp of passion
crossed by the woof of humour, form the texture
woven of the idea, the movement of which they
follow, and with the workings of which they un-
dulate.   Thus developed, they fail naturally of
the definiteness and particularity of the scenes of
Shakespeare, but, when considered secondarily, they

have, in the same degree as the characters, an actual importance. Of this the *Deformed Transformed* affords the best illustration. The idea carries with it the fragmentary scenes, which yet in themselves are often dramatic.

It has been pointed out by critics that Byron's individual characters only appear few and lacking in variety by contrast with those of Shakespeare. This is true, but not the whole truth. Shakespeare's characters, in working out the dramatic end, have been made to show at the same time the traits that mark them as individuals. Byron's characters are the puppets of fate, yet by their very relation to it betray a human side and traits of individual identity. And it is in the suggestive power and freedom with which he bestows these touches that Byron resembles Shakespeare; although, consistently with his method, the circle of his creations is narrower. The types comprised within this circle fall naturally into three divisions — the protagonist, who works out the purpose of destiny; the woman, who reflects the action in suffering; and the minor or accessory characters.

It is in representing the protagonist that Byron's weaknesses chiefly beset him. Stepping into his characters, as every creator must, he is led by the personal impulse to identify himself with each in turn. But he only does this to a *greater extent* than Shakespeare. The disturbing element does not eliminate the artistic element, but contends with it in varying degrees from failure that is never final to success that is almost complete. Manfred, let it be conceded, has much of Byron in him. Yet compare him with such shadowy or melodramatic types as Harold, Juan, Lara, and he gains at once in dramatic force. Go beyond this, and follow him through the mazes of his despair, and he becomes a Hamlet, with all the human significance of the type, and with all the individual reality that a Hamlet so circumstanced would have. If from Manfred we pass to Sardanapalus or Cain or Arnold, the advance in dramatic power is evident. Each of these, besides his typical significance, has the more intimate touches that mark him as an individual, and that vital reality that suggests a world of similar figures beyond him. Cain, the knowledge seeker, has all the tendernesses that belong to husband and father and brother. Sardanapalus revels and fights like "another Antony;" Arnold summons us to another sphere, and his image at once calls up before the mind a series of spirits as chivalric as himself. A similar individuality is perceptible in the characters through whom is developed the darker side of Dipsychus. The scorn of Lucifer differs from the worldly sarcasm of Cæsar, as this in turn from the exultation of the spirits that mock Japhet. Within its prescribed limits, Byron's ironic humour plays with artistic spontaneity. Still more conclusively will the dramatic propriety of Byron's protagonists appear if an attempt be made to transpose them in any way. If Cain be only Byron, let him be supposed the protagonist in the *Deformed Transformed,* and the result will bring to light no mere incongruity of sentiment or environment, but fundamental incongruity of personal identity. Or, as a more crucial test, since the dramas in which they move have a closer resemblance of scene and sentiment, let Cain and Japhet be transposed, and it will be seen at once what nice and clear shades of personal character divide them, what fine conceptive distinctions adapt each of them for his particular part. When all that is personal to the poet has been abstracted from them, there must be claimed for the best of Byron's characters, along with those of the Greek dramatists and those of Goethe, a place, if on a lower pedestal, beside the characters of Shakespeare —first, because of their immense significance as ideal types, and next because of the inexhaustible creative power of which the humanity in them is suggestive.

The women of Byron, beyond all his other creations, embody the paradox of his genius. Beings instinct with passion, they are yet drawn with the most temperate sobriety, the most delicate discrimination. They have all the personal intensity that belongs to their sex, yet their

emotion never raises them out of undue relation
with the larger dramatic conception in which
they move.   And, again, being as nothing, they
are the pivot on which all turns, and while the
victims of man's passion, often prove the arbiters
of his fate.   In all this the natural, unerring
force of Byron's dramatic insight is clearly displayed.   Women are as essential factors in the problem of destiny as men, but under a more special
aspect and with a pathetic difference.   Byron has,
consciously or unconsciously, in common with
Shakespeare, grasped the profound law that,
unless under exceptional circumstances, woman
as an independent existence is non-natural, and
therefore undramatic.   Man alone confronts destiny directly.   Woman must meet it indirectly
through the man, otherwise some chords of her
nature remain untouched.   It is thus that women
stand out as exponents of what is truest and
deepest in Byron's conception of humanity.   The
judgment that could class them as mere Medoras
has been gross indeed where it needed to be

most subtle. If they love, it is because love is
"woman's whole existence," the law of her being;
but it is at the same time only the emotion
through which they gain touch of the human
tragedy. Shakespeare lets this law play beneath
the freedom and versatility with which he approaches all his creations; Byron's application of
it is only narrower and intenser as his method
is more restricted in scope. As his main conception centres in a protagonist who is to be the
interpreter of fate, so to each protagonist he has
"set" a woman, "as perfect music unto perfect
words," to be the finer interpreter of his action
and thus to enhance the moral of the drama.
This has been brought out so fully in the preceding analysis that it is only necessary to refer
to examples. How completely does Myrrha, who
is actually a slave, echo the finer chords of
Sardanapalus's soul until she blends it to the
nobility of her own! How perfectly does Olimpia,
in the brief glimpse afforded of her, strike the
key-note of patrician haughtiness and regal chastity

befitting one who is the heroine in a drama of
earthly splendour, and who was meant, we feel, to
be one in fate with the aspiring humanistic
Arnold! And, to take an inferior example, what
an analogue is the visionary, half-real Astarte
to the abstracted, half-theatric Manfred! That
Manfred's selfishness involves her he loves in
utter ruin is inevitable; but his selfishness has
a kind of ghastly magnificence about it, and
accordingly a certain halo of desolation is appropriately thrown about Astarte too.

But while their emotion is subdued to that
with which it works in sympathy, Byron's heroines,
no less than his men, are instinct with life and
individuality. How distinct, if we carefully study
them, are the springs of action, the ideals, that
animate a Myrrha, an Adah, an Angiolina, though
all are alike in their devotion. And all the
heroines will bear the same test as was applied
to the men. It is impossible to transpose
any of them. Myrrha, for instance, although a
slave, has many points of contact with Olimpia.

Both are inherently noble, both have a steadfastness
that mocks at death, and both have that pride
of personality that marks them out for tragic
issues; yet we have only to imagine their positions
changed to perceive that the dramatic character
of each does not depend merely on the contact
of that conceptive world in which she moves, but
is involved in the personal identity that gives
to that relation its peculiar impress. Byron's
heroines have also, like his heroes, that living air
which argues them but instances from a crowd
alike in kind. Only, whereas the men suggest
types and individuals, the women, consistently
with their nature, suggest rather traits and
characteristics. From characters such as Adah or
Myrrha it is easy to deduce similar personations
of clear-sighted love or steadfast devotion. But
love and sympathy imply also their opposites,
and we may find in Byron foreshadowings of
these as well. In the passionate Marina are dis-
coverable the germs of a Queen Margaret; and
Aholibamah is the stuff of which circumstances

might mould a Lady Macbeth.   The female figures
Byron has drawn are less numerous than the
figures they suggest to our imagination.

On the minor or accessory characters it is
needful to touch but lightly, since to them applies
in a lesser degree all that has been said as to
the leading characters.   If the protagonist and the
heroine are the mouthpieces of destiny first, and
individuals only secondarily, this must *à fortiori*
apply in still greater degree to the lesser persons.
As *dramatis personæ* who assist in carrying
out the main motive, they are perfectly adequate.   But they have also an actual dramatic
reality which might too easily be overlooked
Naturally they have not, and do not require to
have, the force, completeness and variety of the
minor characters of Shakespeare.   They are much
less numerous, and tend to run more ino a few
types.   They are sometimes shadows, seldom
failures.   But few of them are mere abstractions
or even lay figures, and most of them have that
vitality, that abounding naturalness, which is

nothing less than Shakespearian. Watch the
developement, within the restricted sphere assigned
to them, of such characters as Abel, Bourbon,
Arbaces, Zillah, Zarina, and there will appear in
them some dramatic propriety that connects them
with the central motive, together with some personality of trait that gives them individual distinctness.

It has been asserted that Byron was deficient
in the faculties of thought and imagination, a
charge which, if true, would alone be fatal to his
claims as a great poet. After what has been said,
however, it will not be difficult to show that the
allegation rests on a misconception. Byron's
imagination is the same in kind with that of
Shakespeare. It is not in the faculty itself that
his failure lies but in the use and exercise of it.
His . esitancy is the weakness, not of sterility but
of immaturity. Imagination in his hand is as a
god's thunderbolt ; but sometimes the passion in
his eyes confuses him, so that he wields it carelessly, and it misses its aim or even falls short
altogether. Imagination has many sides. Trace

it in Byron, to begin with, under an aspect great but not its greatest; in the ground just traversed— in his dramatization.   In the ease and mastery with which he blends all elements and parts in a rudely organic whole, in the naturalness with which he throws an appropriate atmosphere over each drama, in the spontaneity with which he developes his characters—in all this there is implied dramatic imagination of a very high order.   Where then is its limit?   It is limited precisely as his genius is limited—in actual achievement, but not in potentiality, in possibility of expansion.   The external impulses that forced his poetic activity into intense and narrow channels arrested so far the flight of his imagination, but could not affect its power, which never failed to assert itself as these impulses were more and more withdrawn. As his whole dramatization begins from his personality, but spreads outward so as to embrace humanity, so his imagination begins with sharp reality but expands so as to take in wider horizons. The play of imagination may be compared to the

swing of the pendulum oscillating from the mind
of the poet to that which is external and beyond
him.   In Shakespeare the pendulum is always at
the impersonal extreme; in Byron it stays there
for a shorter time, and often seems to have swung
back. This craving for the fact, for what is per-
sonally known to him, cannot be better expressed
than in his own words: "I hate," he says, "things
all fiction, and therefore the *Merchant* [*of Venice*]
and *Othello* have no great associations for me,
but Pierre [in Otway's *Venice Preserved*] has.
There should always be some foundation of fact
for the most airy fabric, and pure invention is
but the talent of a liar." Saner principle could no
poet lay down than this. Truth is the basis of
the highest imagination.   There was something
in Byron quite akin to the power that could
understand as it had conceived *Othello,* only he
must wield it unconsciously and in his own way.
Let all that has been said as to Byron's dramatization and the conflicting *media* through which
it works to its appointed end be taken as reflect-

ing the mingled strength and hesitancy of the
conception that is creative of it, and Byron's
possession of dramatic imagination, the penetrative
sympathy that can pierce to the heart of a character
or a situation, stands amply vindicated by an
infallible self-record. And yet the vindication
may be extended and Byron's dramatic imagination
summoned to bear witness to itself in another
way. The presence of imagination is betrayed no
less through unconscious indications than in direct
effect. In all great dramatic work there will reveal
themselves to the disinterested seeker, attentive
it may be only to casual beauties, besides the
imaginative play that springs from the prevailing
stress of the poet's emotion, gleams and flashes
of a more spontaneous sort, as it were the by-play
of a mind which, as it is inherently dramatic,
must needs respond to every dramatic impulse,
even though in so doing it may take on forms
which consciously it affects to depreciate or reject
as alien. Most interesting, for instance, is it to
note how, when off his guard as it were, Byron slips,

not of set imitation but freely and spontaneously
into the natural Protean utterance of Shakespeare ;
or how his imagination now and again touches, not
in superficial similarity of phrase but by congruity
of conception, the imagination of the Greek dramatists. Manfred, as he bids farewell to the sun (v.)
is Ajax or any other Greek hero. A companion
situation breathes the same spirit, but with ampler
detail.   Arnold, wounded to the quick like Ajax,
goes through a similar agony of passion, utters the
same affecting farewells, and is impelled to a like
swift, indignant choice of death, even to the setting
of his knife that he may "fall upon it" (vi.).
From the phantoms that shortly after pass before
Arnold, (vii.) the mind may catch the same imaginative effect as is produced by the kings that pass
before Macbeth, but is perhaps more insistently
recalled by them to the forms of those Argive
heroes watched by Antigone from the Theban
walls.   And yet another scene in Arnold's drama

(v.) *Manfred*, Act iii. Scene 2.
(vi.) *Deformed Transformed*, Part i. Scene 1.
(vii.) *Ibid.*

strikes a different note ; for the warriors whose
"glorious, gory, shadowy hands" seem to Bourbon
to beckon to him from the walls of Rome (viii.) are
conceived in the same spirit as those murdered
babes that burst upon the sight of Cassandra
awaiting her doom before the doors of Agamemnon's
palace. A final instance carries us to Euripides
and reveals Myrrha watching beside the dream-
perturbed couch of Sardanapalus, (ix.) like Electra
by that of the frenzied Orestes. Of Shakespearian
passages many have already been incidentally
quoted, but two more may here be given for their
special imaginative effect. In the words of the
archangel Raphael : "True, earth must die . . .
And much which she inherits," (i.) we seem to
hear an echo of those of Prospero. And is it
Charmian or is it Arnold that is saying :

> "Silence ! oh !
> Those eyes are glazing which o'erlooked the world,
> And saw no equal ? " (ii.)

(viii.) *Ibid.*, Part i. Scene 2.
(ix.) *Sardanapalus*, Act iv. Scene 1.
(i.) *Heaven and Earth*, Part i. Scene 3.
(ii.) *Deformed Transformed*, Part ii. Scene 1.

From the imagination as specially concerned with dramatic effect may be distinguished, rising from and blending with it, that which is imagination in the highest sense of the term. Imagination in this aspect becomes the faculty that is intuitive of truth in general; the medium which, vibrating with tremulous susceptibility between the seen and the unseen, can stir in us continual suggestions of " thoughts beyond the reaches of our souls." Imagination in this kind connects itself intimately with a poet's contemplative mood; it is the bloom of his philosophy, and springing from the sphere where his thoughts habitually rest, is ethical rather than dramatic in its scope.

Here, on ground that is familiar to him, Byron's imagination has its flights, and sometimes falls. And here too we may once more surprise the poet talking to himself, and gather from his unpremeditated words a confirmation of the evidence afforded by his work. Side by side with the passage above quoted should be read that remarkable memorandum in his diary which is

again a self-revelation. "What," asks Byron,
"is poetry?—The feeling of a Former world and
Future." In its infinite suggestiveness, in its
realization of the perpetual significance and relation of things, this prose poem of a sentence
seems to contain the pith of the matter, to give
the mood in which high imagination works.
Byron's imagination only wavers as his apprehension of this relation wavers. His drama,
depending as it does on the ethical even more
than on the dramatic end, is perpetually concerned with that relation, at the same time that
his mind in its constant flux and reflux, and
wavering between doubt and affirmation, can
rest in no settled scheme of things. This contradiction is reflected in the wider workings of
his imagination. *Sardanapalus* throughout is
agleam with finer imaginative light, the glow
failing, not from want of innate force, but dwind-
ling as the poet's vision films and saddens. In
Cain and *Heaven and Earth* the imaginative
light plays as strongly but more darkly beneath

the tremendous material issues. In both these
dramas what seems the catastrophe is but as
the break and pause of the cataract as it
disappears over the rocky brink. As the consummated action ends the moral enigma begins,
and the material loss and desolation open up for
the spectator horizons of kindred emotion in the
human soul, which are only contracted in their
sweep by the same accidental conditions as
hampered Byron's conception of the universe and
of humanity.

And, as was the case with the expression of
dramatic imagination, that which, in this higher
imagination, appeals to us by great instances,
may also be traced in passing touches which,
apparent with potential promise throughout both
the poetic and dramatic work, culminate only
in the latter. In many of the invocations to
Nature, in those references to a grander past,
in the more familiar elegiac strains of his poetry,
as in many a scattered note of meditative yearning and pathos and regret in his dramas, there

breathes a spirit which, if not imagination itself,
is the stuff of which imagination is compact,
and which deepens into imagination in those
electric utterances that compress the meaning
of a lifetime into a single line, or make an
exclamation the vehicle of hoarded thought and
emotion. Such are the "Old man, 'tis not so
difficult to die" of Manfred, which forces us to
re-consider the whole scope of the drama of which
it is the epilogue; or the "And with me!" of Cain;
or the "That's hard, poor slave!" of Sardanapalus.
Touches like this are possible only to the great
masters, and there are more of them in Byron.

Again, from the exercise of its highest mood
imagination turns to revel in its own strength,
and then becomes the fanciful or creative imagination, which, by combination of the known and
remembered, can evolve new realms and new forms
which shall be absolutely self-consistent and true
to the nature of their being. And in this sphere
there is no mean possible between success and
failure, for whatever does not commend itself

as true in this kind thereby loses its form and
identity.   Here therefore it is easier to trace
Byron, and here, too, he fails—but only from care-
lessness ; where he succeeds he equals Shakespeare.
How genuinely his fancy works is shown by its
constantly seeking inspiration at a source most
native to his genius.   Whenever his spirit would
find repose or expansion, it is to nature's bosom
that it flies; and here therefore his creative imagination nestles.   The scenery of the dramas has
already been noticed as an effect, but for the
imaginative effort this implies its principal instances may be recalled:—The dream-realm of
Assyria in *Sardanapalus;* the primeval world of
Heaven and Earth; Eden and the abyss of
space and the shadowy Hades in *Cain.* The last
is the greatest instance.   The scenery of *Cain*
is imaginatively so grand that it is justifiable to
speak of a Byronic universe as of a Miltonic
universe; and it may be noted in passing as a
characteristic trait, that while Milton's universe
is elaborated to the smallest detail, Byron's is

displayed by touches and vivid glimpses. And
as with the realms so with the forms of fairy-
land. Relying on the strength with which nature
inspires him, Byron has created one at least
peculiarly his own and worthy to mate with Ariel
or the fairies of the *Midsummer Night's Dream.*
The Witch of the Alps is the embodiment of the
ecstasy felt by Byron in the presence of nature,
the Galatea quickened by his love from the natural
elements into animation and life. The power
implied in her creation escapes us in the effect
of the beauty it produces; and it is a power
which Byron has used with only less effect elsewhere. The angel lovers, Azaziel and Samiasa,
kindle "all the west, Like a returning sunset," and
themselves take on the conception suggested by
the "flashing path" they leave behind them (iii.).
The figure of Lucifer, sombre, faded, yet touching in its fallen magnificence, is made living
once for all in a simile that likens it to the deep
"purple" of an "ethereal night" streaked by the

(iii.). *Heaven and Earth,* Part i. end of Scene i.

"long white clouds" and spangled by "unnumbered stars, (iv.) and gathers largeness from association with the abysses of space. And, on the lower human level, all natural beauties are made to pass into Adah's face, which yet transcends them all, (v.) as the "starry mysteries" are re-pictured in Myrrha's eyes. After nature, Byron has yet another spell to conjure with. He did not possess —any more than Shakespeare—the Greek spirit, but he had, with Shakespeare, what is next best —a sense of the spirit of the antique past, which had so refreshed his poetry; and it is this lustre of the fanciful imagination which he has thrown, with other beautiful effects, over *Sardanapalus* and the *Deformed Transformed*. Besides such successes may be placed a few failures. Byron is too fond of summoning "spirits from the vasty deep," which prove when they appear to be flimsy and theatric, as for instance those caricatured from *Faust* in *Manfred*. But Byron can

(iv.). *Cain*, Act i. Scene 1, near end.
(v.). "My sister Adah. All the stars of heaven," &c.—*Ibid.* Act ii. Scene 2.

stand the comparison, for his worst shows us by contrast what his best is.

To vindicate Byron's possession of imagination is to have defended him against the charge that he could not reason, that he was incapable of coherent, philosophic thought. For the true answer to the charge is that it holds good as against a philosopher but not as against a poet. The philosopher holds truth for one, to be demonstrated coherently in its entirety; the poet, as a mystery of countless aspects, to be presented as they arise; nor, though some of these may clash, is his presentment less true. Some basis indeed of "thought" imagination must have, to be aught but a vagary of the mind, indistinguishable from mere madness. No inspired fool ever wrote a great poem. Still it is not the *primary* function of a poet to think, but to present, and intent as he is on conceiving and representing, he thinks by intuition rather than by a strict process of reasoning. Thus a great poem always presents the abundant food of thought, never a final sys-

tem of thought. The meditative conception comes
first, bringing with it the informing thought, and
the fuller the poet's meditative range, the deeper
and riper the thought it evokes. Now it is only
as a philosopher that Byron fails—*when he reflects
he is a child;* but as poet his range of thought
is only limited by the range of his conception,
which was itself shown to be restricted by causes
accidental rather than essential. But within its
native poetic range Byron's thought reigns supreme.
Whenever his imagination works freely on a motive
clearly conceived, thought is at hand to guide
it lucidly, serenely; he knows precisely what
he would do, his hand never misses its aim; (vi.)
only when, yielding to negligence or promptings
that beset him from without, he turns aside from
the goal and forgets the guiding conception, does
his hand become weak and his thought wander
inarticulate. How naturally does each drama, as
we have seen, gather about itself its appropriate

(vi.) "But whatever [Byron] actually produces is a success; one
may in fact truly say that with him inspiration takes the place of
reflection."—GOETHE: *Conversations with Eckermann.*

note of thought—the philosophic tone native to
its theme; a sure sign of a master spirit! Or, if
a special instance be sought, that of *Cain* will
suffice. When Byron makes his hero argue with
Lucifer on the "double mysteries," he is attempting to philosophize in detail and is lost; but when
he would lay bare to us a soul ardent to know,
yet always baffled—conscious of error, yet haunted
by a rankling sense of injustice—capable of hope,
pity, love, but impelled to hate, rebellion, despair,
and remorse, then his touch is sure, inevitable,
unerring. Cain presents a psychological study no
less perfect, if less complicated, than Hamlet. Or
again, taking Byron's method as a whole, we may
compare it momentarily with Goethe's. Goethe,
knowing well what he would do, makes each line
of *Faust* move, weighted with meaning, to the end.
Byron, conscious also of a goal, but uncertainly and
straying often from the path, sets down many lines,
many passages, of incoherence and inconsequence;
yet continually the leading motive reappears, and
so we get by way of the stars to the end. Goethe—

though even Goethe not without some interrupting interludes—leads us on in luminous, unbroken calm. Byron's mind leaps at the subject and illuminates it by fiery flashes; but the glimpses so obtained are clear and vivid, opening far-reaching vistas of truth.

Is yet another word permissible on this subject? Recalling what was said as to Byron's power to impart imaginative homogeneity to each drama, is it refining too far to say that imagination, in the fusion of *all* its forms, conveys an added something which is as an effect of itself and so beyond it— a charm felt to be indefinable, but which may be expressed as the constant spontaneous play of genius itself upon its material. This is that which greets us all-embracingly in Shakespeare; smiles to us as from the face of a friend in Molière; wins us with mingled austerity and voluptuousness in Milton; steals on us with subtlety in the best modern poetry. It is conspicuously absent on the whole, or present only in a vitiated form, in Hugo, whose passionate rhetoric egoism is jealous of aught

tending to inveigle it from its immediate stress and
aim, and it is absent, in a different way, from all
works which are the result of striving talent rather
than of creative genius. Did Byron possess it?
Had he this last seal of the poetic nature? The
answer is of interest, as concerning an effect
breathed from the very arcanum of great poetry,
and common to all admittedly great poets whatever
their diversity. It will depend moreover on the
care with which we can assert Byron's possession
of such a characteristic relatively to other poets,
and so lead up to that final estimate of his genius
which it has been the object of this essay tem-
perately to enforce and make clear. And this
can best be done here by saying that with Byron
the charm is the flow itself of his genius, gleaming
and sinking as this gleams and sinks, and meeting
or receding so in relation to the ideally best in
other great poets. For in proportion as charm
results from the association of genius with enduring
rather than fleeting interests does it become ideal
in aspect. To this ideality Byron constantly at-

tains; and it is this quality of his art that makes it confluent—always Byronically, always with intermission, always brokenly and by recurrence—with the art consummated in Sophocles, the art that lifted Shakespeare above his fellows, the art that sets Goethe easily at the head of modern European poetry (vii.).

(vii.) Cf. Note at end.

VI.

If the present attempt has succeeded, Byron should stand before us somewhat more explicable than before, great alike in his completeness and incompleteness, his weakness and his strength; no monstrous prodigy who stumbled on greatness by mistake, but a sane poet, working by principle and law. And any importance belonging to this view must lie in the fact that it seeks not to set up a rigid theory, but to show the universal sway or tendency of the poet's genius governing all its diverse and discordant elements as a harmony—not to vindicate Byron as a perfect dramatist, but to show that the qualities elementally present in his poetry spring from a common root of greatness, which does but attain its richest and fullest developement in his dramas. These are the fruit of him, as *Harold*, *Juan*, the *Vision* are the flowers. But the interpenetrating idea that runs through both the poetry and the drama is one—the idea of Humanity.

This claim has never been clearly made for Byron. That which forms his real and indefeasible title to fame has neither been explicitly denied nor adequately affirmed. He has been placed in an indeterminate way above the crowd of poets who are but half-voices, purblind, seeing but shadows:—to set him above these is not enough, he differs from them in kind; and again he has been confusedly admitted into the company of sovereign poets, yet with an implied stigma of inferiority:—this is pure error; he is the same with the greatest poets in kind, and he differs from the foremost only in degree. To use once more, from its peculiar appropriateness, the old grand metaphor—the soul of Byron too has felt immortal promptings, and blundering often at the gates of heaven, has been dragged downward by the mortal steed; yet often, too, they have opened to him, and he has been borne round in the train of the gods and seen in glimpses the fair vision of that which is eternally true. And whensoever he expresses this that he has seen, his matter glows into the unanalyzable tissue of which great poetry is composed; takes on the incommunicable strain which all great poetry breathes. This absolute attainment of the best and highest, so rarely and so hardly reached amid repeated fallings, is the mainspring of Byron's power, the secret of the divinity in his nature that unites him indissolubly with the immortals. He is of them by the quality of his vision, by the same divine air he is capable of breathing, by the residuum of achievement, which, when all his " worser part " has been thrown away, remains of like sort with theirs. He is only less than the foremost of them because he is oftener torn away from the contemplation of the best; because his gaze is less serene and comprehensive; because the glimpses vouchsafed him seem so fleeting and fugitive. Yet even thus he is not far beneath them. For though

his gaze be less steadfast, its motion is swift and
far-ranging in various directions; and though
his glimpses be brief, they are the more piercing
and suggestive. Byron's inspired moments con-
dense so much.

This view is only the consummation of the
theme that has been gradually developing
throughout our inquiry. It is now therefore time
to test the full pregnancy of it by a final comparison of Byron with a few of the names which
are greatest in literature, as well as with some
of those which meet his in a more immediate or
cotemporary interest.

By what quality does he, however unequal, mate
specially with Shakespeare?—By his universality,
the versatility with which his mind ranges over
all the elements of life and nature, fusing them
in the light of an imagination based on truth.
And let it be noted by way of contrast, how in
Marlowe, with whom at first sight Byron would
seem to have far closer affinity, the mighty line,
the stronger dramatic oneness of passion, the in-

comparable poetry, yield before the "various" line, the revealing humour, the wider human outlook of Byron. At what point does he, how- ever inferior to them in a hundred others, touch with such poets as Æschylus, Dante, Milton ?— Partly again, of course, in the breadth and sweep of his vision, but specially in that sublimity of conception which can not only evoke super- human forms, but imbue them with superhuman life and surround them with an appropriate environment. From Sophocles what an impas- sable gulf would seem to divide him ! Yet with Sophocles Byron is assuredly akin in his sym- pathy for the nobility of man and the perception of the "irony" of his fate; as he is with Euripides in his keen sense of the pathos in the lives of men and women. With Alfieri, with Schiller, he breathes now the magnanimity, now the yearning aspirations of the human spirit, and with Goethe, the greatest modern, though it be with less subtle comprehension, he shares that conceptive power which, intuitive of the latest tendencies of time, can give them shape and utterance, and reveal the world to itself in a figure.

If from a general comparison we turn to one more special, which shall confront him with nearer English cotemporaries and on the field of a common rivalry, we ⋅shall find the result no less instructive. Passing by lesser men, and leaving unregarded the arabesque of Moore, the lifeless phantasmagoria of Southey, the harsh transcriptive of Crabbe, we pass at a bound to Scott, only to note how the antiquarianism, the romance, the martial fire and varied picturesqueness of his poetry still leave us on the outside of the human heart that Byron probed; while Scott's epic prose wants the "last touch" of passion to make it dramatic in the Shakespearian sense. And not far off, apart and lonely, is Landor, petulant, humanistic, a scholar, yet with some defect of imagination that leaves the flower of his gifts fruitless, as his temper failed to harmonize the external gifts of fortune. In a

very different group, a triumvirate unlike in
character yet alike in fate, stand Shelley, Coleridge, Keats. To set Byron in true relation with
these poets is to probe and try his genius by
the very sharpest and most intimate test.
And yet the true nature of their mutual relation seems to be always misapprehended, or at
least set forth in a misleading way. It is good
to be a Hugoite or a Shelleyite; to know the
light through contact with any of its beams; it
is still better to be a lover of poetry—the poetry
that is still a-building, and beholding thus
securely every poet in his due relation, thank-
fully to sympathize with them all. To say that,
in such an aspect, Byron was greater than
either of the three is not to disparage them,
but to shed redoubled honour on both him and
them.

There is a power of song, but there is also a
power of flight. And in the ideal poet both
would exist in counterpoise; but under mortal
conditions this happens seldom. And whereas the

latter power necessarily includes something at least of the former, the converse is by no means the case. So that many a true poet, setting to perfect music the thoughts that arise within him, remains, by stress of fate or his own weakness, a potentiality only; (i.) and sometimes a poet, borne on ampler sweep and concentrating all within his glance, misses in his haste the earlier, sweeter music, which may yet come to him later, a recovered gift. Yet surely his achievement is the greater of the two, or, if not greater, more fortunate. And so Byron outsoars those who were his peers or even more.

Shelley has been charged with being too ideal. But can a poet be too ideal? or did Marsyas in truth conquer Apollo? There would seem to be a paradox here, much needing the illumination of some larger truth. Nay more; Shelley is *not* a mere idealist; he is often soberly real, and has a firm hold on *common* sense. We should rather say that he failed to adjust the ideal and the real,

(i.) Cf. p. 152.

and by refusing to serve his apprenticeship to the latter missed also the former. He does not spurn the solid earth, but rejects it as a troublesome formality. Poets will always understand him, but of full success, wherein more is demanded, he fails, except on occasion. In a poem, for instance, like *The Cloud*, where fact and ideal coalesce, the result is pure perfection; whereas in poems like the *Prometheus*, ideal and real float wavering athwart one another, to the discomfiture of the higher imaginative truth. Yet few reading his *Defence of Poetry* can doubt that Shelley would eventually have harmonized his spiritual and material worlds, an orb outshining Byron's. Criticism, however, cannot assert this; it can only assert that Shelley, dying in youth, was a potentiality. Like some wild-eyed tameless hawk he circles feverishly with amazing strength the empyrean, but falls before he has poised his wings for one true, definite, persistent flight.

Keats approaches truth from another side. The magical, natural passion that is the life-blood of the very earth flows in his veins and animates him without effort; yet only exposes him, another Antæus, to nobler defeat at the hands of a power more divine. This is simply Shakespeare's story; and Keats, with an individual difference, "is with Shakespeare." This is no wild error of criticism, but the very truth that trembles from his work for those who incline to its true meaning. Had time allowed it, there is no doubt that Keats would have surrendered up his natural realm of beauty to that ampler spiritual sphere that was ever leaning forward in his soul to meet it—a world out-embracing that of Byron. But though criticism can foreshadow this it cannot assert it. It can but assert that Keats was a potentiality—a poet of song, not of full flight; dead, even while the strain swelled preludic from his lips.

And of Coleridge, our sorrow, our cruel loss, criticism has to say still less, and can but assert that he was scarcely even a potentiality, so strangely does his most complete work reel and waver

before us in its unreality. We see him go forth
a noble vessel with sails full set towards all
continents of truth; but as it goes the ship glides
a phantom into a phantom atmosphere, and floats
on unreal, "wrecked in opium-mists."

If these three had attained each his full flight,
the world should have wondered, and Byron had
been outsoared indeed!

And beside these regal potentialities, place, for
sake of wider comparison, three poets who were
not Englishmen, or in any sense potentialities,
but achievers of the full inspiration that was in
them, and one of them at least a consummate
artist. What a contrast to that of Byron is the
work of the Italian Leopardi! What strength
and nervousness of thought is here, wedded to
an emotion as ardent and sincere, and restrained
by a taste as exquisite! Yet Leopardi, fine artist,
clear thinker, true poet as he is, lies spellbound
within his dungeon of pessimism, a soul cloistered
from that living universe which Byron ranged
with such yearning but not unfruitful thought.

Turn next to Musset, and perceive how in another way this French disciple of Byron is dwarfed beside his master. For the utter lack in Musset of any sense of that larger morality contracts the play of his genuine dramatic instinct, limits the span of his imagination, and reacts upon the puppets it enspheres; a race diminutive indeed beside the larger-statured souls that front the spacial sweep of Byron's mental horizons (ii.). And from Musset the transition is easy to a still more famous if not greater personality; this time no consummate artist, but a poet of as ample sweep as Byron, and weighted by as sinister influences of embittered failure and intoxicating success; as it were a companion-picture, like, yet unlike, and so the richer in the contrasts it implies. For whereas the self-stricken Byron, continually drawn out of and beyond himself by

(ii.) To the names of Leopardi and Musset we may add those of Lamartine, and of Heine, the "German Byron"—the one with his feminine Byronic note of lament; the other with his blended pathos and irony playing fantastic in an unsubstantial air of levity—by way of insisting how far certain elements which constitute Byronism are from accounting, in their sum, for the genius that was Byron.

the constraining conception of a wider human ideal, and advancing with ever clearer spiritual vision, touches and grounds ever and anon on Olympian facts, Victor Hugo, always with some beclouded intimation of those facts, and always shifting like an *ignis fatuus* about and athwart them, with continual glare and Titanic movement and reverberation of verse, never really grounds on them, but, dominating all to a colossal egotism, scantily relieved by enfranchising humour, does but render us a blurred impression of the universe, increasingly bewildered and brilliantly confused.

But yet another poetic English cotemporary, neither a potentiality merely, nor greatly an artist, but more favoured by circumstance and of stead-faster mind, if with less natural gifts, upbuilt, he too, what though with many fallings and falter-ings, the universe anew, and re-sphered it to the world of his imagination—a world full of quiet paths and wayside flowers, yet overarched by a serene sky fading into an illimitable Beyond, wherein men may still roam and find refreshment.

14

Surely it is Wordsworth and Wordsworth only
beside whom we can finally bring Byron to rest
as his peer and co-equal; a greater even than
Byron, perhaps, if one thinks of the grandeur of
his vision and the sublimity of those moments in
which he has made us its temporary sharers.
Yet even Wordsworth is so wrapped in the
beauty of his own dream that his message at
times seems to fail for us upon his lips as
he communes to himself. And is it not this
same Wordsworth of whom his great apologist
has said that his " eyes avert their ken from half
of human fate," so that we are conscious of a
deadness haunting his work, which leaves it
marred, and miss a thousand living impulses
which Byron can stir within our souls? But
such as they are, in virtue and defect, Wordsworth and Byron stand out foremost among all
native cotemporaries—foremost, we repeat, not in
innate, actual possibility of power, but in actual
achievement, in the rounded completeness of so
much of the one true poetic ideal as they were

able to present. In this sense, and this sense only, no third English cotemporary poet can be added to them—perhaps no foreign poet save Goethe—but they shine, the poet of Meditation and the poet of Action, the Dioscuri of the poetical firmament in our nineteenth century (iii.).

But we must return finally to Byron alone. For if this criticism should seem overlaboured, it must be remembered that its aim is not to prove Byron the greatest of all poets, but great *among* the greatest poets, and, through a peculiarity, *uniquely* great among them. It has been asserted that had Byron lived the poetic side of his genius would have merged insensibly into the practical. To this criticism has no answer to make.

(iii.) This judgment, so far at least as concerns English poetry, is due to Mr. Matthew Arnold, who also, in his own way, adduces the parallel of Leopardi. It may be permissible, without over refining, to put the matter more exactly thus: In the field of English literature Byron and Wordsworth stand indubitably at the head of the poetry of the earlier nineteenth century; but on the wider European canvas, Goethe and Byron stand out as poetic protagonists on that as yet dubious interspace which touches clear, in one direction, on the eighteenth century, but has its hither borders shrouded in the shadow and mystery of the on-coming twentieth century.

What it can and does answer is that Byron, as revealed in his extant work, was a potentiality who
was also in a high degree an actuality. And it is
in this actuality that he finds his identity and
his place. Being great among poets, neither ex-
cluding any nor including all in himself, he is
also, we repeat, by a peculiarity, great in a different way from them, and in a more *interesting*
way. Aiming, as it were, at all the stars in
succession, he builds up the universe by fiery
touchings, and so rounds the sphere of thought.
What matter that there are fallings and blank
spaces of darkness? for by these touchings he
comes in contact with the divine gulf stream of
poetry, and therein participant with all great
poets, is in his strength and weakness less than
they all and greater than they all. For whereas
each may surpass him in some special measure,
his imagination seems momentarily vivid at more
points; and these points are mostly of a poignant
human interest, and are further intensified as
by throes of his personal sufferance. Proved, he

is easily found wanting; yet the most relentless analysis but lays bare in him an indestructible quality of greatness. He is in very truth the least of all poetic apostles—is literally not meet to be called an apostle; yet, by virtue of the human stress within him, that Pauline enthusiasm to which all secrets of man and nature fly open, the greatest of poetic apostles (iv.).

This is the open secret of Byron, and this, I think, was the meaning more or less consciously present in Goethe's clearly brooding mind when, probably without reservation, but in the full natural sense of the terms, he spoke of Byron as different from all other English poets, and in the main greater. But the "super-eminence" is but the impression made on a great and thoughtful mind by a character so rare, so startling, so fascinating. Enough for us to make for Byron the claim of "eminence among the eminent." Par-

(iv.) In another connection we may say Byron is Euphorion — precisely that Euphorion whom Goethe painted; the embodiment, viz., at a particular moment, in wondrous, *interesting*, albeit imperfect form, of that eternal spirit of poetry of which Goethe himself was the ampler cotemporary manifestation.

ticipation in the life-stream so few explore was
his; his feet are constant by its shores, and his
emotion, rushing forth to mingle with it, reissues
as an image of the universe glassing in its aspect
the larger meaning of men's lives. Against a
power such as this, breathing with elemental
vitality from within outwards, the criticism of
impulse or the criticism that is apprehensive
merely of accidentals beats and shall beat idly, a
mere babble of dilettanteism.

And still, at whatever risk of tediousness, a last
word, and that not the least important one,
remains to be said of Byron. Those subsidiary
human ideals, which are not necessarily poetic,
but which poetry more and more tends to absorb
into herself, occupied no small place in his mind,
reacting with decisive influence on its more purely
artistic developement. And this it is that links
him strangely to us by the bond of a still-pulsing
interest. Let us, then, fearlessly and consistently,
from a point of view that considers him in the
light, not of a rigid theory, but of a tendency,

follow him for a moment into the might-have-
been—the realm foreshadowed larger of traits
existing in his actual work—and so bear his fame
on to a level far higher than that assigned to it
by his wisest and most discriminating critic.   For
not only is a poet greater than his work, but his
ideal is greater than the poet, and thus the
possibilities that it suggests are really a portion
of his inheritance to us, the orbit to which it
enlarges our mental sweep.

He is "the passionate and dauntless soldier of
a forlorn hope;" "He has no light, cannot lead
us from the past to the future."   In the clear light
of facts it is not thus we read Byron.   It is true
that, dying at thirty-six, he lacked culture and had
not "the artist's nature and gifts;" but he had
the insight, more priceless than culture, that is
eagerly assimilative of new truths, and a genius
that was its own earnest of perfection.   In this
he was a poet for all time.   But the peculiarly
interesting point about Byron is that to the
possession of those gifts which make him a poet

of all time he added the possession of those more
special ones that make him the representative
poet—as Byron, and not as Goethe—of his own
time and of the time immediately succeeding.

Goethe might strike his hand unerringly upon
the sorer places of humanity and say, "Thou
ailest here and here;" but Byron, taught by
personal sufferance might with equal truth say,
"I *feel* that thou dost indeed ail here—and
here—and even here!" Thus, if he could not
actually lead us, he has indicated the true way.
If he sheds no light on the problems that most
intimately affect us, he faces them sensitively, yet
fearlessly; and this is to initiate their solution. He
was a bard or prophet who dimly felt the stirring
of hopes no longer now forlorn; and so far from
the light within him being darkness, it was just
the definiteness and true imaginative reality of
his intuition that gave his poetry that actuality
the attainment of which circumstances alone
denied to the probably greater poetic genius of
Shelley or Keats or Coleridge.

At setting out this essay found the name of Byron inextricably associating itself with that of Goethe; and in this final inquiry we shall have chiefly to suggest how Byron sunders from Victor Hugo, the latest navigator in such seas, and follows in the wake of Goethe, steering away from mirage towards truth.   The prospect is a tempting one, but we must dismiss it with a glance.

As we found that a noble seriousness or morality amplified and enlarged Byron's artistic world, so we find those narrower aspects in which humanity can be regarded illuminated in him by a quality which we may term humanism.   And what we note generally in his humanism is that it is strengthened by humour and good sense and practicalness, in contrast with that humanitarianism which is sickly, spurious and sentimental.

Amongst those subjects of perennial human interest, which are as elements that poetry combines, politics in its ideal sense is one of the highest. Of Byron and politics we may assume all has been said.   But here we have to ask what is its mean-

ing, its significance. How precisely are Byron's
so-called unpatriotism and cosmopolitan sympathies
analogous with his "critical" position in things
literary! It is the unpatriotism that alone is
spurious, the sympathy that alone is real. What
Byron here sees with his flashing instinct is the
self-seeking, the hypocrisy, the idolatry of what is
lowest in the national ideal; and instinctively rushing blindfold against it, and carried away into saying
far more than he means, he disparages his country
with impulsive exaggerations easy to understand.
But his sympathy was genuine, and assuredly em-
braced his true country—the country which in his
day was but emerging—in its fitful but instinctively
true love, initiating the path which those who love
England and humanity would fain have England
follow now. And with Byron's wider political sympathy compare Hugo's too fervid Chauvinism, embittered as it was by cruel circumstance, flattering
where it should have warned, centering blindly on
one point, and failing to purge its noble enthusiasm
by any keener fires of thought; and then note how

the impulsive intimations of Byron coalesce with the slowlier conceived political ideals of Goethe.

Compare in the same spirit Byron's attitude towards the more complex issues of society. What we have here to note is his democratic instinct combined with aristocratic hatred of that vulgarity which it is the misfortune of liberty at the outset to set free. Here, too, Byron's impulsive fitfulness is the more apparent as the problems to be solved are more complicated. But observe how true that instinct is. Byron coincides with Goethe and men of steadfast thought in taking the larger view of social problems as not simple—as including many diverse elements; and so doing deviates as far from Hugo, whose equally sincere instinct is allied with childishness, ignoring true difficulties, seeing but one aspect, slurring over all anarchic elements with a film of sentimentality.

Religion covers another large province of human thought. See once again the impulsive Byron ranged on the side of the clear-sighted

Goethe. See once again his spurious "critical" position in regard to the religious question. Full of the poet's religious instinct, he shrinks from the superstition encrusting older faiths, yet half falls back upon them through reaction; hesitates not because of cowardice, but from pure doubting-ness, from scepticism. All this is the old "un-criticalness" over again. But on the poetic side, on the side of the stress of his elemental poetic thought, he cuts sharp through all superstition, towards science, in the direction of Darwin and the clear truth,—wanting only larger knowledge. Compare the position of Hugo, starting it may be with the like true instinct, but playing about the subject with amiable personal fantasy, and directing to a different goal—is this through some likeness of national strain?—a stream of subjective analysis which recalls the insaner mystical side of the philosophy of Comte.

The qualities I have provisionally summed up as humanism—the yearning to living, actual men; the yearning to truth, to active endeavour; that

passionate contempt for much that is implied in
the term "literary" which characterizes every
poet in proportion as he is great—all these
qualities round the portrait of Byron, and unite
him indissolubly, as I have said, with Goethe,
as unlike within like. Not in vain has it been
said of Byron (v.) that he did not, as a poet,
sum up any *national* epoch. But he did have,
as we know, a full sense of the antique past
and an intuition of the as yet distant future.
And just as this makes him a fitful-winged
herald of the world-literature about which
Goethe dreamed, so does his humanism ally him
with Goethe in an intuitive dream of that
coming era of thought, in which alone a world-
literature could have place. Goethe looked with
comprehensive glance; but within this radius
worked the intensive eagerness of Byron too.
Goethe wrought comprehensively and with intention; Byron with true instinct and too fitfully.
Those who would adventure on that new era

(v.) By Professor Elze.

must embrace an ampler ideal even than
Goethe's, and must learn of Byron as from one
that failed rather than as one that succeeded;
yet none the less they must call Goethe father
and confess Byron as a pioneer. On the shore
Goethe stands, beaconing away from himself.
Byron is seen a little distance off, striving
stormily, hindered, in the same direction. Looking on him it is as if we saw a noble vessel
entangled in some narrow firth of error, beaten
against the rocks, smitten by the blasts, heaving
restlessly, yet ever slowly forging right on, and
showing in every sweep of her not ineffectual
agony, and by every strain of her bending masts,
how mighty a yearning is hers for the open sea
of truth, and how triumphantly she may yet
ride it. Let it be remembered that Byron was
faithful to humanity with his latest breath. That
final expedition to Greece was the most Byronic
act of his life. Discount all the posing, all the
sick restlessness and ambition of it, and there
still remains about it a certain perfume of

nobility. And the reason is that it was but his attempt to realize the ideal that lay hidden at the root of his poetry, his practical testimony to the truth faintly adumbrated in *Sardanapalus* and writ large in the Second Part of *Faust*— the truth that humanity must renounce in order to attain; must die if it would live again; must suffer practical regeneration before its transmuted elements can pass into new ideals of thought and action. This is the allegory of the NOW in which we live. Let us project thither the shadow of the Byron we have attempted to describe, and so leave him.

Born into our freer and more tolerant co-temporary air, the genius that was Byron would have fronted the world with spirit renewed and refreshed like the eagle's. The old problems would have lain before him deeper and darker, but their stress would have been lifted from himself, and their solution have appeared not impossible in the light of a dawning knowledge. In this serener atmosphere his revolt must insensibly have won its way to that reconciliation towards which, as we have seen, it was but a continual aspiration; his unquiet scepticism have been quickened into larger faith; his personal passion transmuted into a more purely human emotion. Nature would have allured him with her old solace, but he would have often turned from her to let his fancy play with kindlier satire, with more genial sympathy over the world of men. The mind that was passioned for reality and loved "something craggy to break upon," must have owned the spell of science, yet none the less used her ennobling flame to re-light the torch of poetry. Freed from the conditions that thrust it back upon itself, who can doubt that the mind of Byron, straining resistlessly in all directions, would have touched at every domain of human thought and mastering, not o'ermastered by, the complexity, harmonized the wealth so gained in the unity of a richer, a mellower, a more contemplative imagination? Such a spirit could never have rested in the sublime pessimism of a George Eliot; the virile resignation of a Matthew

Arnold; the faith grasped through shadows of a Carlyle. Sharing something perhaps with Browning, rivalling on different lines and carrying forward on other levels the unapproachable work of Tennyson, Byron must have pressed onward to a place unfilled and reserved for him alone. Working in the spirit, not the letter, on the principles, not the exact procedure, of Shakespeare, it, is scarcely prophesying to assert that Byron's genius, which circumstance alone obstructed, must, unimpeded, have reached that full expansion of which his actual work was the rich immature promise, and that, if not in dramas, in still nobler dramatic poems, he would have revealed as in a figure to the perturbed age the very form and pressure of itself, and dowered the world with a later *Faust*.

It does not seem certain that the time has even yet come for that final recognition of Byron which, passing by all factitious accretions of praise or blame, shall be content to rest on his genius in its simplicity; but it must come soon. When it does come, all that was but the cotemporary

glamour of his verse will have disappeared; and
with it, alas! the living voice that spoke, with
whatever exaggeration, to living cotemporaries.
And what remains, too, will have suffered diminu-
tion—the inevitable touch of languor and decay
that time lays on all things; but it will be the
immortal part of him, his poetic contribution to
the spirit of Humanity.

NOTE.

—

A PASSAGE in Grote's *History of Greece*, descriptive
of the expansive spirit breathed by the Athenian
dramatists into the precedent Greek poetry, seems
to me so applicable that I here transcribe it; especially as it enforces an aspect of Byron's mind
which I would particularly· emphasize, and further
suggests his relation to the Greek drama itself.
The primary phase of Byron's dramatic genius is
the delineation—born through self-suffering—of a
soul spiritually at bay. He not only delineates
a Prometheus or an Orestes, but himself *is*
Prometheus, *is* Orestes. We must be more than
careful, however, not to confound him with this
narrower phase. For Byron, if not myriad-minded,
is truly many-sided, and we shall find him—a fact
which cannot be too much insisted on—rising, by
a higher developement, to that dramaticalness of

imagination distinctive of Shakespeare, and, by yet further developement, to that *modernness* of imagination distinctive of Goethe.

The passage from Grote is as follows:

" The great innovation of the [Athenian] dramatists consisted in the rhetorical, the dialectical and the ethical spirit which they breathed into their poetry. Of all this, the undeveloped germ doubtless existed in the previous epic, lyric, and gnomic composition; but the drama stood distinguished from all three by bringing it out into conspicuous amplitude, and making it the substantive means of effect. Instead of recounting exploits achieved or sufferings undergone by the heroes—instead of pouring out his own single-minded impressions in reference to some given event or juncture—the tragic poet produces the mythical persons themselves, to talk, discuss, accuse, defend, confute, lament, threaten, advise, persuade, or appease—among one another, but before the audience. In the *drama* (a singular misnomer) nothing is actually done; all is talk, assuming what is done, as passing or as having passed elsewhere. The dramatic poet, speaking continually, but at each moment through a different character, carries on the purpose of each of his characters by words calculated to influence the other characters and appropriate to each successive juncture. There are rhetorical exigencies from beginning to end; while since the whole interest of the piece turns upon some contention or struggle carried on by speech—since debate, consultation and retort never cease—since every character, good or evil, temperate or violent, must be supplied with suitable language to defend his proceedings, to attack or repel opponents, and generally to make good the relative importance assigned to him, here again dialectical skill in no small degree is indispensable.

"Lastly, the strength and variety of ethical sentiment infused into the Grecian tragedy is among the most remarkable characteristics which distinguish it from the anterior forms of poetry. 'To do or suffer terrible things' is pronounced by Aristotle to be its proper subject-matter; and the internal mind and motives of the doer or sufferer, on which the ethical interest fastens, are laid open by the Greek tragedians with an impressive minuteness which neither the epic or the lyric could possibly parallel. Moreover the appropriate subject-matter of tragedy is pregnant not only with ethical sympathy but also with ethical debate and speculation. Characters of mixed good and evil, distinct rules of duty, one conflicting with the other, wrong done and justified to the conscience of the doer, if not to that of the spectator, by previous wrong suffered—all these are the favourite themes of Æschylus and his two great successors. . . . The tragedian not only appeals more powerfully to the ethical sentiment than poetry had ever done before, but also, by raising these grave and touching questions, addresses a stimulus and challenge to the intellect, spurring it on to ethical speculation.

"Putting all these points together, we see how much wider was the intellectual range of tragedy, and how considerable is the mental progress which it betokens, as compared with the lyric and gnomic poetry . . . which formed the glory and marked the limit of the preceding century. In place of unexpanded results, or the mere communication of single-minded sentiment, we have even in Æschylus, the earliest of the great tragedians, a large latitude of dissent and debate—a shifting point of view—a case better or worse, made out for distinct and contending parties—and a divination of the future advent of sovereign and instructed reason."

GROTE : *History of Greece*, Part ii. chapter 67.

THE END.